Pat Thomson

Strange Exchange

BARN OWL BOOKS

First published in Great Britain
by Gollancz in 1991
This edition first published 2002 by Barn Owl Books
15 New Cavendish Street W1M 7RL
Barn Owl books are distributed by
Frances Lincoln

Text copyright © Pat Thomson 1991, 2002
The moral right of Pat Thomson to be identified as
author of this work has been asserted

ISBN 1 903015 17 0
A CIP catalogue record of this book
is available from the British Library

Designed and typeset by
Douglas Martin Associates
Printed and bound in Great Britain by
Creative Print and Design Wales, Ebbw Vale

Strange Exchange

Mike worries about whether he is going to be able to cope with his French exchange student. He would be worrying even more if he knew the truth. Pascal comes from a distant planet. And what is Pascal to make of Mum's exploding dinners and Dad's attempts to speak French? The alien finds the world fascinating but is shocked at the violence he encounters and just has to do something about Bazzer and Gav, the class bullies.

In the end Pascal decides that human life is very funny and very serious, often at the same time. But friendship can hold it all together.

Other titles by Pat Thomson

For Susanna

Chapter One

PASCAL STOOD BY the pulsing screens watching the succession of figures bringing him nearer and nearer to his task. His thoughts of home receded into the vastness of space behind him. Earth lay ahead, and there he must carry out the duty assigned to him. The Navigator Senior at the console spoke, never taking her eyes off the screen.

'You are fortunate, Young One,' she said. 'You have been singled out – you alone – to do this task for us. You will become part of our planet's history. Only one as young as yourself could gather the information we need without arousing suspicion. Are you not proud to serve your people in this way?'

'Excuse me,' said Pascal. He took a deep breath. 'I think I'm going to be sick.'

One hour nearer Earth and feeling steadier, Pascal sat in the cabin of the Senior Captain, receiving his final briefing. He tried to explain.

'It's just motion sickness, Sir. I get it on my hover-bike occasionally.'

'Did the Central Committee know about this?' said the Captain. 'I hope they know what they are doing. You understand what is required? You will appear at the rail-way station at the exact moment that the chosen host family will arrive in order to collect a foreign student.

We have diverted the student – a minor viral infection, puzzling to Earth doctors but harmless. Letters will be sent but they will not arrive. The family will collect you, and, for a period of Earth time, you will monitor the thoughts of the members of the family. After that, more complicated work may follow, but we shall see.'

'I understand.' Pascal nodded.

The Senior Captain closed his eyes briefly.

'I wonder if you do?' he murmured. 'We have been monitoring Earth for many years. There have been crises before. They learn little from history. They seem so un-controlled, there is no order. Now we fear they have the power not only to destroy themselves, but to create an imbalance in the universe. We shall begin to infiltrate. We have not entirely decided how to do it.' He looked quickly at Pascal and then looked away again. 'You are in the nature of an experiment.'

'I don't think I can save the universe,' Pascal said humbly.

'That will not be required. You are just a monitoring device, nothing more.'

Pascal thought about it. The whole idea seemed less exciting than it had in the training laboratories.

'But this Earth family, they must suspect me, surely?'

'I think not. You have been thoroughly trained, fully informed. And anyway, it is an English family and they will imagine you to be French. The English will believe anything of the French. That is one aspect of human behaviour we must try and understand.'

'At least I can keep my name, Sir.'

'Yes. Strange that your name is so suitable. You were fortunate to be named after an old programming language. Rather sentimental, but useful. It seems that Pascal is also an appropriate French name.'

The bleeps on the scanner rose in pitch. The Senior Captain stood up.

'Good luck, Young One,' he said, 'or should I say *bon voyage!*'

'Pardon?' said Pascal.

At the station, the Castle family waited. Mike wondered why he'd ever filled in the form. Half the holidays taken up with looking after a stranger. What if the French boy didn't like England? What if he was keen on ballroom dancing? Mike had a cousin who was keen on ballroom dancing. He even cleaned his shoes before he danced!

Mum was anxious, too. She kept saying extraordinary things, like they would all have to have proper breakfasts, instead of running round the house carrying cereal bowls or toast. Dad was really relaxed, though. He was looking forward to it.

They were coming through the barrier now. A woman with a kind smile etched into her features was pairing them all off. Mike half hoped they had sent a girl by mistake. He took another look and decided he couldn't cope with any of these and settled for anything reasonably human. A vibration ran momentarily through the metalwork of the station. They all turned, expecting to see a train moving out, but nothing was happening. As they turned back, the still smiling woman grabbed a small, dark-haired boy and said, 'You must be the Castle family's guest. Welcome to England.'

The Castles shuffled forward and they all smiled kindly, too. It might have been a smiling competition.

'Bonjour, son,' said Dad. 'This is Michael and this is Madame Castle. Now where's your luggage?' He picked up the boy's silvery bag and led the way to the car.

In the car, Mike tried desperately to think of something to say. He would ask if the boy had had a good journey.

'Did you have a good journey?' asked Mum.

'Thank you. I did,' the boy answered. His accent was slightly foreign but very good.

'I don't speak French very well,' blurted out Mike.

'Never mind,' said the boy. 'I will speak your language.'

'Now then,' laughed Dad. 'Mike has to parler the old Français a bit, too, you know.'

'Of course.' The boy nodded and looked out of the window.

'That's the gasworks,' said Dad. 'Quite a well-known landmark.'

'Well, not well-known, exactly,' said Mum.

'It is to us,' said Dad. 'I'm just showing him the sights. That's the post office. The main post office,' he added.

'Thanks, Dad,' Mike murmured under his breath.

'We'll take you out and about a bit,' said Mum, looking at Dad and frowning significantly. 'We're taking a few days' holiday. And I hope you'll get to like our English food.'

Mike gulped. Mum was very interested in food. She was trying to be more creative, she said. For lunch, they had experienced Liver Meringue Pie. Pascal was listening and nodding politely. 'Pauvre petit Pascal,' thought Mike, with a flash of inspiration, but he could hardly say it out loud.

The car turned into the close and pulled up outside Number 17 Worcester Way. It was an ordinary estate house. Quite pleasant, but ordinary. Pascal, however, was looking at it as if he had never seen anything like it before.

'This is your house?' he asked.

'This is *la maison*,' confirmed Dad.

'It is not a house, then?' Pascal looked puzzled.

Dad did not hear. He was opening the boot and taking out the silvery bag.

'You travel *lumière*,' said Dad jovially.

As they walked up the path, the door opened and Liz stood on the step.

'Thought I heard you. Come on in. I'm Mike's sister. You must be Pascal.' She shook hands and led the way indoors.

'You and Liz give Pascal a tour of the house and settle him in his room,' said Mum. 'I'll get the meal on the table.'

'*Exactement!*' beamed Dad. '*Naturellement!*' He looked pleased with himself and added, '*Quelle bonne idée!*'

'Come on, Pascal,' said Liz, giving Dad a withering look. 'Your room's up here.'

Pascal had the spare room. The sewing machine and the unused exercise bike had been moved out and Mike had put up a poster of French cheeses on the wall to make the room more friendly. Pascal moved around as if he were learning the layout.

'This is the window?' he said.

'You have windows in France, don't you?' said Mike.

'Don't be silly,' said Liz, 'he's practising his vocabulary.' She went round the room, helpfully naming objects. 'And these are curtains,' she said. Pascal looked blank. 'To pull across when it's dark.'

'Ah yes.' Pascal brightened up. 'It is dark at night.'

Liz giggled. 'You sound like a phrase book. The bathroom's opposite.'

Pascal seemed fascinated by the bathroom. He picked up toothbrushes and tried the taps. Mike felt a little uncomfortable but Liz was cheerfully conducting a language exercise, pointing and naming and giving explanations in a slow, loud voice.

'Shall we help you to unpack?' she asked.

'No, no,' said Pascal. 'I will go now and unpack. It will not take long.'

'We'll see you downstairs, then,' said Mike. 'Tell us if you need anything. Make yourself at home,' he added, feeling mature and responsible.

They went downstairs.

'He's OK,' said Liz. 'I like him.'

'What shall I do with him?' asked Mike. 'Ten whole days!' He felt desperate.

'It's no big deal,' said Liz. 'He's here to experience English family life. He's not royalty. Just treat him like a normal human being, that's all you need to do.'

That night, Pascal lay on his bed. He was wearing the light cotton suit Supply Senior had called pyjamas. He was also wearing a fine chain around his wrist. It was silver, with one bronze-coloured link. Putting his finger on the link, Pascal pressed gently. The chain began to glow a little, then brighter and brighter, until the bronze link was a tiny pin-point of piercing light. Pascal turned the chain and projected the light against the wall. Immediately, a large screen lit up and an Information Senior looked back at him. Pascal tuned in his thoughts and began to receive.

'All goes well, Young One?'

'I am well.'

'Domestic information is good. We have clear pictures of the house and implements. This, however, merely confirms what we already know. Tomorrow, we shall try and use your hands as special receptors. Shake hands with everyone – you remember how to do that? And touch everything. You must get closer to the boy. So close, that we can read his thoughts. Who is the girl?'

'She is his sister. That is to say, she and Mike have the same parents. Her name is Liz.'

'I understand. Also study her. So far, there are two problems. The food does not entirely conform to our Earth food information bank. It is rather different. And language.' The Senior frowned. 'The language conforms except for the father. We have no record of this pattern.'

'I cannot understand him, Senior,' Pascal admitted.

'We will help you to work on this problem,' replied the Senior. 'It may be that he is some kind of hybrid. Not quite human. Contact us again tomorrow night. Now we will give you sleep. Rest.'

The light faded and Pascal closed his eyes before sleeping. He remembered they had told him to do this and obeyed.

Mike sat up in bed, sucking the end of a pencil. He always wrote his diary in pencil in case he felt differently about things later on. He sometimes felt quite embarrassed about his past. Like the time he had sung

All Things Bright and Beautiful over the goldfish's grave. Not as embarrassed as when Dad tried to speak French. What could he do? Pascal obviously didn't understand a word. Pascal seemed all right, really. A bit quiet. Still, who wouldn't be quiet after Mum's supper?

'Tonight,' he wrote, 'Pascal's first night here, we had beef boiled with marigolds or something. I think there were peanuts, too. There were hard bits, anyway. Pascal is OK. Liz was nice to him. Dad is not OK. He thinks he is Napoleon. I have to stop him somehow. Think I will have breakfast before Mum gets up.'

Mike sighed and put his diary away. He wondered if it would ever become an important historical document like Pepys's Diary. He closed his eyes and went to sleep.

Chapter Two

MIKE WOKE UP with an uneasy feeling. At first, he could not think why. It was the holidays; it wasn't his day to clean out the rabbits. Then he remembered Pascal. It wasn't that he did not like him. He did. It was just the terrible responsibility. All this having to entertain him and protect him from the family. What if he thought all British people were like the Castle family? There might be a Third World War. Then, he also remembered the wedding.

'Mike! Mike!' His mother was tapping on the door. 'Look after Pascal, love. I'm just off to the hairdresser's. Won't be long.'

Mike pulled on his dressing-gown in honour of Pascal's presence and went downstairs. Liz was making tea.

'Lucky old us,' she sighed. 'Dear Cousin Joanie's wedding. Seems a terrible thing to do to our guest.'

'Mum thought it would be a good experience for him. She keeps talking about British life and customs,' said Mike. He sighed.

'He'll certainly see some of that sort of thing,' agreed Liz.

Dad came in. He looked equally glum.

'Cousin Joanie's wedding,' he said.

They all fell silent. A teaspoon swished in the cup. Cereal popped intrusively.

'Why! Here's Pascal!' Dad suddenly bellowed. Liz and Mike jumped. Dad leaped to his feet, beaming. 'Well, well,' he said enthusiastically, '*Dormied bien*, then?'

Pascal smiled equally brightly and thrust out his hand. Dad looked at it as if he wasn't quite sure what to do with it.

'Oh yes!' said Mike. 'French people always shake hands.' He came forward and Pascal shook hands energetically, first with him and then with Dad and Liz. He was very thorough and even patted Liz's hand as well which she thought rather touching. He then went on to pat the table, the chairs and the toaster.

'Ah, you want toast!' said Dad triumphantly, as if he had just interpreted the needs of a dumb animal. They settled down to toast and marmalade and Dad took Pascal into his confidence. 'Afraid we've got something on today, Pascal, *mon* old *vieux*,' he said.

Pascal eyed Dad's open-necked shirt and cords.

'Yes?' he said.

'Got to go to a cousin's wedding. My wife thought it would be interesting for you, you see. It *will* be interesting, of course,' he said, trying to be positive.

'If he's into pink satin and Uncle Roger's jokes,' said Liz.

'I wear something special for this?' asked Pascal.

'No, no,' said Mike hastily, 'not pink satin. We just look tidy and that.'

'Just brush your hair and you'll look a million dollars beside my brother,' suggested Liz. 'It's OK, really. We go to the church, have a bit of a party afterwards and then come home. With a little luck, we don't even have to speak to Joanie or the poor mutt she's marrying.'

'Now, now,' said Dad. 'At least Pascal will get the chance to meet all the family.' He smiled benevolently around the table. Liz smiled back, less benevolently, while Mike's face registered a kind of desperate fortitude. Pascal stared back at Dad solemnly. It was, Dad thought vaguely, like staring into the lens of a video camera.

They were still slopping comfortably around when Mrs Castle got back from the hairdresser's.

'You're not ready! We've got to be at the church in an hour.'

Mike and Pascal dressed in record time but they found they were simply in Mum's way.

'Why don't you lads walk on ahead?' suggested Dad sympathetically. He had just pressed his new silk tie on 'very hot' and Mum was scraping the bottom of the iron. 'Your Mum's like a cannon gone loose on board the *Victory*. Oh,' he said, quickly, 'not the Battle of Trafalgar, of course. I meant the Battle of . . . erm . . .'

Fortunately, Pascal did not seem to have noticed. He followed Mike out of the gate and they started to walk down the road.

'Now what is this wedding?' asked Pascal. 'What is it for?'

'But you have weddings in France.' Mike was surprised. 'You know, *mariage*? Or is that something you don't really see in the desert?' he added, frowning.

'We go to the desert?'

'No, no. A wedding is when two people set up home together.' Mike paused. Actually, it was more complicated than that. He sighed. Now he needed a degree in sociology.

17

Pascal put his hand lightly on Mike's arm. Mike looked at him, but Pascal smiled suddenly and seemed to understand.

'Ah yes. It is a new family grouping, is it not?'

'Exactly.' Mike beamed and then Pascal saw the smile fade and the colour leave his face. 'Here comes someone I don't want to meet.'

Pascal saw two boys approaching. They were both large. One had a broad face and was grinning widely. He wore huge, metal-tipped boots. The other was sharper; big but neat and restless.

'Bazzer and his sidekick,' muttered Mike.

As they met, the two strangers blocked the path. Mike and Pascal stepped to one side, but the other two did the same.

'Oh dear,' said Bazzer, 'they don't seem able to get past. What shall we do, Gav? How can we help?'

'Push 'em in the face,' suggested Gav.

'Gav, Gav, you are so limited. You're frightening Castle. He doesn't look well.'

'Just go away,' said Mike. 'We're not interfering with you.'

'Who's your friend?' asked Bazzer sociably.

'He's a frog,' said Gav. 'That exchange.'

'I might have guessed,' said Bazzer. 'A little froggie friend. Well, you can tell, can't you? It's obvious. A nasty little runt, like all frogs. Can't stand them myself.'

'How would you know?' Mike's voice shook slightly. 'You've only been on a day trip to Calais.'

'Getting brave, are we?' Bazzer took hold of Mike's shirt at the throat, and then looked past him. 'You got lucky,' he said, 'but we'll see you later,' and jerking his head at Gav, he crossed the road and they both walked unhurriedly away.

Mike turned and saw the rest of the family hurrying towards them. Mrs Castle glanced at the retreating figures.

'I do wish you'd choose nicer friends, Mike,' she complained.

They arrived at the church at the same time as the bride. Mike was relieved. They didn't have to talk to relatives, just slip in the side-door and join the congregation as they stood for Cousin Joanie and Uncle Roger. Neither of them looked familiar. Cousin Joanie was actually smiling graciously. He half expected her to hiss 'Push off, kid', when she reached him, like she usually did, but she was like a figure on a cinema screen, remote from her audience. Uncle Roger was not smiling. Although his clothes looked very smart, he gave the general impression that nothing he was wearing fitted him. He walked as if his shoes belonged to someone smaller. His collar troubled him. He kept lifting one shoulder. Uncle Roger had class, Mike decided. Joanie was starring in a soap opera but Uncle Roger was having a go at *The Hunchback of Notre-Dame*.

Mike began to make a calculation. He wondered how many people were like him, not actually wanting to be there. As he worked it out, he felt Pascal's eyes on him and almost felt that his guilty thoughts had been discovered. His guest was giving him his full attention. Mike hesitated, and then handed him a hymn book.

Perhaps I'm socially inadequate, he thought, reflecting on his lack of family feeling. Yes. He'd try that in his diary tonight. He'd been wondering for some time if he was socially inadequate.

In fact, the wedding was better than Mike had expected. Everyone seemed grateful for the diversion a stranger provided and Mike was genuinely pleased to see Pascal received in such a friendly way. Little Cousin William said, 'Don't like yer' when he was introduced, but as he said that to everyone else, too, Mike felt it didn't count. For his part, Pascal was very co-operative. He shook hands with absolutely everyone, including the waiters and the photographer. The photographer, in fact, was so taken with him that he let Pascal take a photograph. The wedding party shrieked and cheered and Pascal was clearly delighted.

'Primitive. Fascinating,' he murmured.

'What does he mean?' asked the photographer.

'A make of French camera,' explained Dad confidently. The meal wasn't bad either. Mike realized that it meant they would miss a meal at home and cheered up quite a lot. They sat at a long table and Mike began to tell Pascal about the family, as they sipped the soup. Another cousin sitting opposite was introduced and described at length his last holiday in France. Mike noticed that it was actually a description of how the cousin's car had performed so Pascal didn't get a chance to say much.

'Got to Dover in one and a half hours flat,' he said. 'No trouble with the ramp, but didn't fancy the way we were supposed to park on board ship. A real risk to the paintwork, I thought.'

Mike's eyes glazed over until he saw that Pascal was looking with close attention towards the far end of the table. A strange wave motion had started. One by one, guests who had been slumped forward comfortably on their elbows or leaning back negligently in their chairs, were starting up, sharply. A hubbub broke out as Mike, fascinated, followed the wave round the end of the table and watched it approach. He had heard of such things at football matches. Then the cause trotted into view.

Little Cousin William was circling the table, behind the guests' backs, sticking a fork into each one and getting a satisfying, positive response. Pascal looked thoughtful.

'The small child is a problem-solver,' he ventured.

'He's caused a few problems,' Mike countered.

'His solution was inappropriate because he is not fully developed socially, but he solved his problem. He was bored.'

'I think he is going to solve it all over again. He's heading for the piano.' They watched William toddle towards the instrument, a purposeful look on his grubby face.

'Let's get out of the danger zone,' said Mike. 'I want you to meet someone.'

They went over to where Mike's grandfather was sitting. He waved when he saw them crossing the room and Mike waved back. He had a special feeling for his grandfather. Grandad didn't say a lot but he was always a comfort.

'This is Pascal from France, Grandad.'

'Glad to meet you, son. How are you enjoying your stay in this country?'

'I am very pleased to be here,' Pascal said politely. 'Everyone is most kind.'

'We're a mixed bunch,' smiled Grandad, 'like every-one else, I suppose.'

Mike could not help himself. 'Too true,' he said. 'A couple of yobs from school tried to cause trouble on the way here. We were just minding our own business and they threatened us.'

'What happened?' asked Grandad.

'Mum and Dad arrived, otherwise it might have been nasty. Honestly, Grandad, what can you do with people like that?'

Pascal was listening so attentively that Mike regretted his outburst. He had probably alarmed him.

'Funny lot, humans,' Grandad said. 'I suppose we have to accept that some human beings never learn. The rest of us just have to make up for them.'

Pascal leaned forward and Grandad smiled at him.

'Saw a lot of your country, Pascal, during the war. There was a family in a farmhouse. They were very kind to us. I've never forgotten them. We needed each other then. Still,' he said, 'it will be very different in the future. All these exchanges and all the frontiers disap-pearing, you young people will live in a different world all right.'

Mike looked at Pascal. His eyes were fixed on Grandad as if he were recording every word.

'I shall think about what you say,' Pascal said solemn-ly. Grandad looked slightly surprised but was obviously pleased.

'Will you, lad?' he said. 'Well, come and see me. Mike will bring you over.'

Dad interrupted them. 'Here you are. Come on, come and enjoy yourselves. We're having a few songs round

the piano. Ooh la la,' he added, to everyone's mystifi-
cation. 'Your Auntie Sybil is going to play for us.'

Grandad looked at Mike's face and grinned.

'Don't panic, lad,' he said, patting his shoulder. 'I saw
your Cousin William near the piano. He dropped that
fork into the works. They won't find out what's wrong
with it for a while yet. We should get away safely.'

That night, when the glowing screen lit up, the
Information Senior was pleased with Pascal.

'You do your work well, Young One. We begin to get
closer to the mystery. The celebration was interesting, of
course, but we already have much information on trib-
al customs. Who were the two young humans you met
on the way to the ceremony?'

'They attend the same school as Mike.'

'He knows them well?'

'He knows them but does not like them.'

'There was a strong feeling of fear.'

'I felt it strongly, too.'

'Where were the frogs?'

'Ah,' said Pascal, 'I cannot understand this. I looked
everywhere. There were no frogs.'

Information Senior was silent for a moment.

'They were hostile to you. It was almost as if they
hated you.'

'I do not understand this either. They do not know
me. I never even spoke, yet there was this senseless feeling against me. And I think they could be dangerous.'
Pascal had worked it out. 'If Mike felt so much fear, it
must be because these boys can harm him. If they
threaten me, shall I stop them?'

'Certainly not.' The light on the screen intensified for a moment. 'Continue to think logically, please, as you were taught. Such an action would expose your mission. You must find human methods.'

Pascal wondered what these human methods might be. He remembered to close his eyes when the screen faded, but he was glad that sleep was sent. He had the feeling that otherwise, this problem might have occupied him all night.

In the room next door, Mike was drawing two columns in his diary. He labelled one GOOD and the other BAD.

'GOOD: all meals out today. Dad had plenty of people to talk to. Nobody kissed me. William sabotaged the piano so Auntie Sybil couldn't play or sing and he was sick on that posh cousin's Porsche.'

He smiled at the memory but then rubbed that bit out. He felt, on mature reflection, that it was in rather poor taste. Then his smile disappeared as he wrote, 'BAD: met Bazzer and Gav. Think they'll try and get me and Pascal. Don't know what to do.'

He also wrote, 'Am I a wimp?' but rubbed that out again, too. Better not to actually write these things. It made them seem only too possible. He sighed. He added, 'And the barn dance is still to come. Another of Mum's ideas. Think I will have breakfast before Mum gets up, tomorrow.'

He closed the diary and lay down, but Bazzer crept into his head and squatted there until sleep finally came.

Chapter Three

MUM WAS UP long before Mike the next morning. She was already in the kitchen, singing a vigorous hymn all about doubt and sorrow.

'You're early, dear,' she said. 'Must get Pascal a proper cooked breakfast. He'll think I'm neglecting him. It's kedgeree – kippers, hard-boiled eggs and rice.'

Mike had heard of kedgeree but he felt sure no milk or sugar was required with the rice.

'French people don't have much breakfast,' he said, making a last effort to stave off disaster.

'But we do.' Mum was firm. This was strange, really. Mike couldn't remember the last time they had all had a proper breakfast. 'Why don't you both come round and see Uncle Roger today? Or we could go shopping.'

Mike snapped fully awake.

'Thanks, Mum, but we won't have time. Got a busy day. Lots to do.'

Mum looked surprised but pleased.

'You've got something planned? Good. What are you doing?'

'Well,' said Mike, 'Pascal has things to do. He has to –' he looked at the kitchen cupboards for inspiration, 'he has to get presents to take home. And . . . and, we're going to see a film with Liz this afternoon.' Liz would back him up.

'Don't forget the barn dance tonight. I've told everyone our French guest is coming. Do you want some sandwiches to take with you?' she continued.

'Don't worry, Mum,' said Mike hastily. 'I'll make them.'

'One thing about you,' said Mum approvingly, 'when you want food, you always get it yourself. Some lads want waiting on hand and foot.'

Mike smiled nobly and started making cheese sandwiches. Pascal and Dad walked in from the garden.

'*Bonjour*, all,' said Dad.

'Hello,' said Pascal.

'We've been having a little chat,' beamed Dad. 'Pascal is very interested in the garden and the way things grow.'

'I have seen many things,' confirmed Pascal very seriously. 'You put them in the ground and they grow.'

'Ah yes,' Dad nodded sagely. 'Lovely bit of soil round here.'

'There is no roof?' asked Pascal.

'You mean a greenhouse? I've got a little one but mainly we just plant out in *le jardin*, wait for *la pluie et le soleil, et voilà!*'

'It is neither too hot nor too cold?'

'Yes, all the time,' said Liz who had just come into the kitchen.

'Don't confuse the lad,' said Dad. 'He likes to learn.'

Mike felt Pascal was incredibly ignorant. He must live in a flat. Probably didn't even have a window-box. He realized that he didn't know anything about his guest. He had said nothing about his family or his home.

'What about you?' Mike asked politely. 'Have you a garden?'

Pascal shook his head.

'It would not be practical,' he said. He paused. He seemed uncertain how to go on.

Mike noticed that he often paused like that. He was working things out in English, Mike decided. He was doing very well. Far better than Mike could have done in French. And Dad was obviously flattered by his interest.

'What are you two doing today?' Mr Castle asked. 'Can I take you anywhere?'

'Can you give us a lift into town?'

'*Naturellement*,' said Dad.

'Oh Dad, you can't really speak French,' sighed Mike.

'Of course I can!' Dad was indignant. Then he caught sight of his breakfast as Mum put it on the table. '*Mon dieu!*' he breathed. '*Qu'est-ce que c'est?*'

'Wow!' said Mike.

They had a morning to get through before they met Liz. They spent most of it in the record shop. Pascal seemed really keen to find out all he could about the current scene. He knew a little but did not seem to understand the difference between classical and popular music. Mike tried to explain, but he was afraid he had left Pascal with the impression that Mozart was in Beethoven's band so he stuck to the modern music and concentrated on giving him a taste of as many good groups as possible. They were thrown out in the end.

They went to the park to eat their sandwiches and then decided to top up with Coke and chips. While they ate, Mike broke the news about the barn dance.

'Pascal,' said Mike, 'I'm really sorry about this, but

Mum wants you to see all our customs and all that so we have to go to this barn dance tonight.'

'A barn dance? What is that? We go to a barn?'

'Well, no. It's in the church hall and it's all country dancing. That sort of thing.'

Pascal nodded.

'I have heard of this. Arms and legs are moved in a jerky rhythm, and then you lie on the floor . . .'

'Help, no!' interrupted Mike. 'Don't do anything like that. It's more like team games. We stand in two lines, then . . .' What on earth did you do? Mike was baffled. 'Well, we just sort of fight it out.'

Pascal did not seem at all worried. Mike had to admit that he was an easy guest. He did not smile much but he seemed willing to try anything. He even seemed grateful.

'You are most kind to take this trouble. I want to learn everything.'

'What about you?' asked Mike. 'What do you like doing at home?'

Pascal considered the question carefully. Watching him, Mike smiled to himself. He's really old-fashioned, he thought. Anyone else would just say 'mucking about'.

'I like mucking about,' Pascal said.

The coincidence gave Mike a slight shock.

'I like your sister,' Pascal said suddenly. 'She is kind. You do not quarrel, I have noticed.'

'Well, not much. Especially not in front of guests,' Mike admitted. 'I suppose we all get on quite well. Mum and Dad are a bit funny.' He laughed. He realized that if they had not been his parents, he would have quite liked them. 'I suppose I've got oddities, too. At least Mum and

Dad have a bit of personality.' It was strange. He had never thought of his parents as people before. It was having an outsider around that did it. 'What about your family?'

Pascal, who had been listening intently, leaned back, away from Mike.

'My family is not quite the same,' he said, 'but I have good support. Shall we go and meet your sister?'

Liz was waiting outside the cinema, as arranged. She had agreed to come in response to Mike's manic signalling with his eyebrows. No one had any idea which films were showing. It was *The Jungle Book*, again.

'Hello, you guys,' said Liz, indicating the posters. 'This will be the sixth time. Do we go in?'

'Is this all right?' Mike asked Pascal.

'*The Jungle Book*.' Pascal read the title carefully. 'It is a natural history film?'

'You must have Walt Disney in France,' said Liz. 'It's his cartoon of the book. Haven't you seen it?'

'Never,' said Pascal. 'It is a film about a book?'

'Yes, written by a famous author called Rudyard Kipling. It's the story of a child in the jungle who is cared for by the animals, but it's not quite like the book. The bear sings.'

Liz looked at Pascal curiously. He seemed to recognize Kipling's name but obviously needed time to get to grips with the singing bear.

'By Rudyard Kipling,' repeated Pascal. 'He was a famous national poet, is that not true? A singing bear,' he said thoughtfully.

'*The Sound of Music* is being revived at the other cinema,' Liz volunteered.

'Liz! You wouldn't!' Mike was distraught.

'This is a bad film?' asked Pascal.

'We keep seeing it on television,' explained Liz. 'It's more singing but not a bear this time, a nun. Can't think where a nun learned songs like that. There's this singing family and the Nazis.' Liz embarked on an explanation. 'It's essentially about . . .' She looked at Mike for help. 'What is it actually about?'

'Don't ask me,' said Mike. 'Sort of being free to sing wherever you like, I suppose.'

Liz burst into song, but only got as far as *The hills are alive* – when a hostile glare from the commissionaire caused her to stop abruptly.

'Are you going to stand outside all day advertising our rivals?' he asked bitterly.

'Let's just go in,' said Liz.

Pascal seemed amused by the cinema. His eyebrows went up and down as he looked at the ticket machinery and the seedy but flamboyant foyer.

Liz grinned.

'How do you like lurex tartan? Bright, isn't it!'

Pascal looked at her steadily and gave one of his rare smiles. 'I am prepared for pleasure,' he said bravely, 'but what is this unusual floor covering?'

'I'm afraid it's popcorn,' said Liz as they crunched across to the double doors.

Once inside, both Liz and Mike sensed a sudden movement from Pascal. He was looking at the screen and fingering a chain he wore on his wrist. They guided him to a seat and sat down. They exchanged glances, unable to exchange comments. Liz had a strong feeling that at that moment, Pascal was lonely, perhaps even homesick. She put her hand on his arm and gave him a reassuring smile. Pascal turned his large eyes on her. It was almost as if she had spoken and now received an answer.

Liz wondered why they ever came to the cinema in the afternoon. It was full of small children with a lot of surplus energy. The two in front of them were tipping their seats up, sitting on them, and then crashing down in unison. One turned and gave them a long, disapproving stare, turned back and put on a pair of sunglasses.

'Don't ask me to explain all this to you, Pascal,' Liz sighed, but Pascal was clutching the arms of his seat as the lights dimmed and the big rectangle of light glowed. The image projected on to it was their local carpet store. A beaming salesman assured them that they would find carpets and service like his nowhere else, and Liz believed him. It was followed by advertisements for half the high street but all the characters portrayed, posing winsomely by fast cars and three-piece suites, were rather more glamorous than any Liz had observed in the actual shops.

'This is not the jungle,' observed Pascal.

'Coming next,' Liz assured him, over the continuing din.

Then the music started and some of the audience stopped rushing up and down the aisles and sat down to watch. Liz could see Mike slumped in his seat, totally relaxed, and gradually, she saw Pascal relax, too. She noticed how he watched the audience as much as the screen. By the time she offered him some popcorn, he was obviously feeling more at home.

'Don't give him that popcorn,' said Mike. 'They make it out of old tickets.'

They came out of the cinema in good spirits. Liz sang and Mike weaved his way rhythmically along the pavement, snapping his fingers. Even Pascal had got the smile sorted out and was inclined to use it.

'We eat before we go to the barn dance?' he asked.

Mike's high spirits subsided instantly.

'Yes, we'd better go home for something.'

Pascal made a long speech. 'I must buy you a meal. It is to be my –' he thought hard, 'treat,' he said triumphantly. 'That is possible? Can you have a telephonic experience with your mother? Then we go to the dance.'

Liz burst into laughter.

'Thanks very much, Pascal. That's really nice of you. Let's go to the Burgomaster. There's telephonic experience equipment there.'

The Burgomaster prided itself on being nice. They made you wait to be shown to a table even if the place was empty, just to show the customers they were not having any nonsense. It was bright and clean and played music quietly. Mike's mother always complained that she could not quite put a name to any of the tunes, even when they came round for the third time. Mike had never heard of any of them. Pascal looked round, nodding. He seemed more talkative.

'I always imagined your churches to be like this. Brightness, quiet, music, ushers.'

'We're a bit early,' Mike told him. 'You should see it

later.' He offered him the menu.

'I thought a burgomaster was a senior official in a town,' Pascal said, looking at the cover.

'No telling what's in these burgers,' answered Mike. 'Good chips, though.'

Liz came back from the phone.

'Everything in order. What are we having? Shall it be the Green Ecoburger – the midget meat with half a cabbage, or the Heart Attack Special – still midget meat but smeared with processed cheese and accompanied by carbohydrates which have known the glories of ancient grease?'

'I cannot find these,' said Pascal, running his finger down the list.

'She means do you want it with salad or chips. It's all the same, really.' Mike was philosophical. 'I'm just going to have chips. They always do a good supper at the dances.' He looked out of the window. 'Let's get a move on,' he said.

As Liz gave their order, he stared out at the shoppers. The crowd parted for a moment and he saw two figures on the other side of the road, leaning on a shop-front. They were Bazzer and Gav.

Chapter Four

WHEN THEY CAME OUT into the thinning crowd, Liz and Pascal were almost chatting. Mike was silent. Bazzer and Gav were no longer there but Mike realized he had become an object of interest to Bazzer. He was Bazzer's holiday entertainment. Gav was easier to understand. He was not very bright. His dad beat him up. His only hope of being noticed was by fighting. That he could do – he had the right qualifications for that. Bazzer was just strange. He enjoyed causing fear and pain. He didn't even seem to mind being on the receiving end. Mike usually kept out of his way but he could see that Pascal was a target Bazzer would like. He was small, harmless and foreign. Bazzer had great contempt for foreigners. Apparently, they were all the same; there were no good ones, and Bazzer had an offensive adjective for every nation. Mike smiled to himself despite his worries. It was laughable, really. What would foreigners think of Britain if they judged it by Bazzer?! All the same, the church-yard was dim and unfriendly and they were just about to cross it.

They were lucky. They were early for the dance and several people were hurrying across from the car-park to the hall, carrying covered plates and dishes. They called out to Liz and soon she and the boys were moving chairs into the hall. Liz introduced Pascal to everyone and an epidemic of hand-shaking broke out. As

34

they ranged the chairs against the wall, Mike apologized again for the dance but Pascal was clearly able to accept all circumstances with good grace and looked around with apparently genuine interest. Mike looked, too, seeing things as Pascal must be seeing them.

The hall seemed stark and bare. On the stage, two elderly gentlemen were talking to a young girl who was seated at the piano. Every now and then, one man polished the top of the piano with his sleeve and pulled faces at himself in the reflection. The only hopeful sight was a long table covered with a white cloth, rapidly being filled with food.

Mike's parents arrived and people drifted over to chat to them, being jovial with Mike and asking Pascal how he liked England.

'Very much,' said Pascal. 'Tonight, I look forward to something different.'

'It will certainly be different,' said one of the men. 'Look out for Mrs Derwentwater.'

There was no mistaking her when she came. Mrs Derwentwater was technically quite elderly but Father Time was obviously not quite ready to tackle her. As she swept to centre stage, the three musicians stood up quickly, straightening their backs and knocking their chairs over. She was wearing a tweed skirt, a festive blouse and carrying a violin.

'I've got me fiddle chaps,' she boomed. 'Let's get on with it. Form sets for *Lady Huntingdon's Posy.*'

'What is this posy?' asked Pascal.

'No idea,' said Mike glumly.

'Two boys over there, not dancing,' bawled Mrs Derwentwater. 'Whip 'em in, somebody.'

They were herded into a set. Mrs Derwentwater raised her bow and the results were unbelievable.

The musicians, under her direction, needed no feeble amplifiers. Fast, loud, rhythmical music filled the hall. For the boys it was like being kidnapped by goblins. They were pushed this way, pulled that, dragged up the set and thumped down it. Red-faced men hissed 'This way,' panting ladies swung them remorselessly. Mike was twirled round and round by a deceptively slight young woman, apparently with qualifications in caber tossing. If she let go too soon, he could see himself tracing an arc across the hall and crashing out of an upper window. A long, final chord gave just enough time for everyone to rush round and get back to their right places, pretending they had been there all the time.

'Who won?' asked Pascal eagerly.

There were cheers, applause and signs of general collapse.

'Don't sit down,' called Mrs Derwentwater. 'Just getting started. Form two straight sets for *Whack the Rowan Tree*.'

In the next hour or so, Mike tried everything. He tied his shoe-laces fifty times, visited the cloakroom, engaged total strangers in ardent conversation, but they still made him dance. He wondered if young people had heart attacks. He was even glad when the country dancing changed to the easier barn dances. Mrs Derwentwater took no part in these tame proceedings, taking the opportunity to refresh herself so she could return to the fray with redoubled energies. By the time supper was announced, Mike was exhausted and determined not to go through with the second half. Pascal, on the other hand, was as excited as Mike had ever seen him.

'An amazingly high level of physical activity,' he said.

'You can say that again,' moaned Mike, so Pascal did, adding, 'much better than a machine.'

'What? Oh, quick, join that queue or the sandwiches will have all gone. Look, do you mind? I'd like to go after supper.'

Pascal shrugged. 'As you wish. You are tired, perhaps.'

'Tired? I'm destroyed. I'll tell Mum and Dad and we'll drift off.'

They came out into the night, Pascal alert and talkative and Mike half amused but worn out. He was just explaining about raising money by holding dances when Bazzer and Gav stepped out of the shadows.

'Been to church? You and your little froggie friend?'

Pascal looked behind him. Gav, mistaking his motives, closed in behind him.

'You've been getting a little too big for your boots, Castle. Answering back. And I don't like foreigners, anyway, especially short, dark little frogs.' Quite deliberately, Bazzer spat at Pascal.

Mike was horrified. He felt sick, yet he could not move. Bazzer had his hands behind his back. Slowly, he brought out an aerosol can. Paint. Mike couldn't believe he was going to use it, but Bazzer suddenly whipped the cap off. In the same moment, he heard Pascal shout, 'Run' and Mike saw him throw his arm up.

Mike did not wait. He belted towards the gate. He heard Bazzer screaming, 'You fool!' and, turning his head, saw first Pascal close behind him and then, lying in the path, further back, Bazzer and Gav. They had apparently crashed into each other. Mike was bewildered but did not pause. With Pascal, he ran out of the churchyard and into the street. They stuck to the well-lit main road, still hurrying, until they reached the estate and a last sprint brought them home. They fell into the front hall.

Mike slammed the door and lay on the scratchy front-door mat.

'I'll never get over tonight,' he groaned. 'I should take more exercise.' He was shaking but tried to hide his feelings. 'You must be in training.'

Pascal seemed unaffected by the physical strains of the evening but he knew exactly what had happened.

'Why do these boys attack us?' he asked, coming straight to the point.

'Oh, they just pick on people,' mumbled Mike.

'They seem to hate me,' Pascal stated simply.

'I can't explain it.' Mike was embarrassed. 'I know it's stupid. I don't know why they behave like that but they are not good people. We're not all like that. Look, Pascal, I'm really sorry.'

'It is not your fault,' said Pascal and held out his hand. Mike shook it and felt a bit better.

'I'm going to have a shower and go to bed,' he said. 'What with Bazzer and Mrs Derwentwater, the world is full of tough guys out to get me.'

'You are making a joke,' said Pascal solemnly and gave a very little smile.

Mike said good-night, knowing that nothing was settled but he just felt out of his depth. He did not feel comforted again until he began to write in his diary.

'Terrible evening,' he wrote. 'I am in a bad state.' He suddenly thought how similar this was to Captain

Scott's diary and felt a little better. 'I may not be alive when you find this diary. I am under great strain but I will try and leave an accurate record.

'The day began well. Although Pascal doesn't seem to have ordinary interests, he doesn't mind taking part. He is always willing to muck in.' He rubbed the last sentence out and substituted, 'I would describe him as mature, I think.' Here, Mike sucked his pencil, despite the evil-tasting eraser on the end. He was reflecting. 'He is clever and doesn't go out much when he is at home. He probably mixes mainly with older people. I am sure he had never been to a cinema or hamburger place before.' Mike felt rather proud of this piece of psychological analysis. The diary was bringing out his natural sensitivity and acute judgement.

'The dance was awful.' His feet were back on the ground. 'The average age was ninety-three. Mrs Derwentwater could flatten a sumo wrestler with one finger. Pascal didn't mind as much as I did. I expect they do a lot of folk dancing in France. The food was good, anyway, and we didn't have to eat at home.' He remembered about leaving a truthful record for historical purposes and added, 'Well, maybe it wasn't that bad, but what followed was awful.' He began to write faster, no longer being the diarist but writing what he really felt.

'Bazzer and Gav really have it in for us. I'd heard stories at school but didn't really believe them. Bazzer must be mad. What's wrong with being French? I wonder if being prejudiced means that you've got something wrong with you and you have to take it out on other people? Pascal was OK, though.' He thought back. What had happened exactly? When Bazzer threatened them,

Pascal threw up his arm and Bazzer and Gav collapsed. Bazzer obviously blamed Gav but what had Gav done? Mike was sure he hadn't touched Bazzer. Mike thought over that awful moment again, tapping the pencil on his teeth.

Suddenly, he bit it so hard that he nearly swallowed the eraser. He saw the arm movement again, clearly. Pascal had done it! He had knocked them both down – but without touching them!

Pascal's day was not ending satisfactorily, either. The screen had exploded into life and a Senior had filled it immediately.

'Today, you have shown the self-control of a human being.' The pressure in Pascal's head was painful. 'Your processing seems to have been inadequate. You had instructions. You disobeyed them. We are questioning your suitability for this mission.

'I did not mean to disobey.'

The Senior found this unsatisfactory. He filled Pascal's head relentlessly. 'Why did you deviate? You know any physical harm can be repaired, even from this distance.'

'That is effective for me. Not for Mike.'

The blazing screen dimmed very slightly. The Senior's thought-waves accelerated but they were less pressing.

'You did this to protect him?'

There was a long pause.

'I tried to disguise my action,' Pascal volunteered at last. 'The hostiles blame each other. Mike was too worried to observe clearly.'

'That is by no means certain.'

The Senior was not convinced but something had

captured his attention. Pascal realized that he was interested in what he had said about Mike. Could it be that some kind of change had taken place? Suddenly Pascal felt nervous. Perhaps this mission would change him for ever. Make him unfit to return.

'I shall not question you further. There are aspects I wish to discuss with colleagues. You must do nothing, I repeat nothing, except collect further domestic information until I speak to you again. How fortunate that these humans need sleep. You, however,' the pressure inside Pascal's head returned, 'do not. Tonight we will run further training sessions. You obviously need them.'

For the rest of the night, Pascal watched the training videos: The Violent History of Earth. Pascal felt very low. Then they ran The Construction of a Primitive Mutual Support System and he realized that it was a family; what the Castles were – what he was in now. He watched it attentively. They had most of the details right but it was somehow all wrong. They had seen but not understood. Humans were variable, each different from the other. They changed according to how they were treated. The Seniors didn't understand how complex as well as primitive they were. Pascal was sure that it had something to do with unprocessed feelings. But what were these feelings? Did humans themselves understand them? Pascal decided that the Seniors thought humans were animals with technology but he was beginning to think there was something else, though he had no idea what it was.

As the screen faded, Pascal became aware of the brilliant light at the window. He got up and pulled back the curtain. He saw Earth's sun. Although he did not quite know why, he found himself smiling.

Chapter Five

'RISE AND SHINE. Show *une jambe*, there!' Dad was calling up the stairs.

When they came downstairs, both Mike and Pascal were glad that there was something definite to do. Today, all the students involved in the Exchange Scheme were to meet in the school and take part in special activities. They set out together, neither saying much.

Pascal thought alternately of the discovery he thought he had made about human beings and his own situation. He was sure the Seniors had failed to understand. The human world did lack order and logic. It was full of primitive technology, inconsistencies and unnecessarily complex feelings. But humans had something else, he decided. It was an emotional dimension which each human being controlled personally and this provided checks and balances. Sometimes it had bad results, but sometimes it produced some of the best things. Yet, how had he gained this insight? Was he becoming more human? If so, could he return home? He tried to calm himself by remembering the thinking exercises he used to do when he was younger. He must gain command over himself again.

Mike avoided looking at Pascal as they walked silently along the road. He felt slightly uneasy but a little foolish at the same time. Last night, he had felt certain that something very strange had happened. In the daylight, it didn't seem possible. Pascal was just a boy from another country. There were bound to be some differences. Then he saw Pascal as he had been last night, his hand raised, his fingers spread, a look of calm authority on his face and Bazzer and Gav grovelling on the ground. It *had* happened, and it wasn't normal.

They turned in at the school gates. Groups of people were milling round. Voices were loud. Showing off was rife. A brand new, continental coach waited for the afternoon's special trip.

'Mike! Over here.' It was Fraser King. A group from Mike's year were standing around Fraser who was acting as some kind of Master of Ceremonies, handing out the name tags. Mike suspected that this public-spirited gesture was a way of getting to talk to the girls.

'Come and meet the rest. This is Ben and Jacques, Smithy and Jean-Bernard, Carol and Sylvie.'

An outbreak of hand-shaking greeted the introductions. Mike said, '*Bonjour*,' and Pascal said, 'Hello'.

Mr Rossiter, looking out of the staff room window, was moved to remark that these exchanges did their bit for World Peace.

'I feel, in a small way, like the United Nations,' he said modestly.

Mr Dewsbury, who was not optimistic by nature, pointed out that it was always the UN who were shot at by both sides. He advocated getting everyone in while the goodwill lasted.

It was strange to be in school when it was so empty. They clattered through the echoing cloakrooms into the hall. Mike realized that Mr Rossiter was serious about welcoming the guests when he saw comfortable chairs, biscuits and Coke. There were even flowers on the stage.

Some of the French students were chatting to each other but Pascal sat by Mike, quietly observing the others. Fraser, on the other side of Mike, indicated Pascal.

'Studious type?' he whispered.

Mike nodded.

'Mine's not. Pierre likes discos. I'm worn out already.' He slumped dramatically in his chair.

'What?' said Pierre, cheerfully. '*Fatigué?* Tired?'

'Sit up, silly boy,' said Sylvie, poking Fraser in the back.

A mixture of French and English flowed back and forth. Single words, strong accents. Mistakes and corrections. Pascal doesn't speak like this, Mike was thinking. He seems unfamiliar with English and yet he doesn't make mistakes. And there's his accent. It's very slightly different but it doesn't sound French. He looked sideways at Pascal. He was looking at the screen at the end of the hall, quietly fingering the chain he wore on his wrist.

Mr Rossiter strode on to the platform, smiling broadly. Mr Dewsbury and Mrs Wagstaffe preferred to lurk just inside the door with two strangers.

'It gives me great pleasure to welcome you here today. A very warm welcome to you, our French guests. And to our own students as well, of course,' he added as an afterthought. 'Let me introduce you to the members of staff.'

The two strangers were French teachers who were also on an exchange and they said in impeccable English how delighted they were to be there. Mrs Wagstaffe waved and smiled from the doorway. Mr Dewsbury sighed and lifted a hand in a movement which suggested that whatever happened it would not be his fault. He was but a plaything of fate.

'We have a great day for you today!' continued Mr Rossiter. 'first, a film from the National Tourist Office.'

Fraser raised his eyebrows.

'This is too much,' he murmured.

'Then the discussion groups.'

Mike vaguely remembered signing a list on the notice board. Channel Tunnel, was it? The Economic Community?

'Then, after lunch, a trip to the museum, and, VERY special this one, a civic reception. Tea with the Mayor, no less!' He smiled triumphantly.

A few whistles and cries of 'Wow' greeted this announcement and Mr Rossiter seemed quite gratified with the response.

'We'll all get together again at the end of the visit,' he continued, 'for the farewell disco, but remember, the main thing is to get to know each other. That's what it's really all about. Right. Ready, Mr Dewsbury?'

'What?' asked Mr Dewsbury.

'The film.'

'Oh. Right.' He made his way to the projector. 'Tom,' he said, 'do you know how this thing works?'

Tom Seymour fortunately did and soon *Great Britain in Technicolor* began to roll.

With the advent of videos, they did not often have films these days and everyone had forgotten about the need for black-out. Great Britain's beauty spots were consequently rather pale, and several members of the audience decided to follow the instructions about getting to know each other, rather than risk eye-strain. The film closed with a stirring military band, marching down The Mall, so the members of the audience were able to stamp in time to the music and restore their good humour.

Mike had hardly seen any of it. There was something different about Pascal but nothing which offered proof of any definite kind. Yet he was beginning to wonder if he was actually French. Looking round the room, he could see that not all French people were the same, anymore than all British people were. He tried to think about what made Pascal different. It was the way he took in information, he decided. His powers of concentration were unusual. He almost seemed to be able to read your thoughts.

Mike jumped as Pascal touched him gently on the arm. They were all moving out of the hall and into the corridor.

'We should be going into this room,' said Pascal, looking at him gently but anxiously.

Mike turned in at the door blindly and sat down in the nearest seat. Pascal sat next to him. He hardly noticed Mrs Wagstaffe's friendly enthusiasm as she got the group going, feeding facts, figures and vocabulary, challenging unsupported opinion, drawing out ideas.

'And you, Mike? You're the only one who hasn't given an opinion yet. Are you for the enlargement of the Community?'

Mike stared back in dismay. He remembered he'd done some notes, talked about it in class. A kaleidoscope of thoughts and views whirled in his head. He could say nothing.

'Mike and I feel there is a more important question.'

Pascal's voice spoke precisely, on Mike's behalf. 'We look forward to an increase in contacts of all kinds that are peaceful. But are we well-enough prepared to take advantage of them? Shall we not just take our prejudices through the Tunnel with us? How shall we change our heads as well as our habits.'

'Er, that's right,' said Mike. 'It's not enough to know, we must understand,' he added, and he knew that the thought was Pascal's.

Despite the pessimistic tone, Mrs Wagstaffe positively beamed.

'Well done, boys,' she said. 'You've been thinking about this. And you,' she leaned forward and read Pascal's label, 'you've been practising, Pascal. Very fluent! Well done!'

'Yes,' said Sylvie, taking up the question. 'I had many wrong ideas. The British are not what I expected.'

'Aren't I?' asked Fraser.

'You especially,' laughed Sylvie, hitting him playfully with a substantial pencil case.

While Fraser uncrossed his eyes, they all exchanged examples of misconceptions, laughing and protesting. Mike looked at Pascal.

'Thanks,' he said. Pascal shrugged and smiled.

After lunch, they piled into the coach for the trip to the museum. Pascal seemed extremely interested in the vehicle. He asked questions about every detail. Mike answered with a cheerfulness he did not really feel. It was, after all, a French coach.

The museum, rather to Mike's astonishment, was a great success. He had never visited it himself and was amazed to find that it was more like a theatrical event.

Expecting rows of glass cases, he was surprised to find himself in a 'time capsule'. Journeying back through time, they passed objects which indicated the retreating centuries, and then burst suddenly into another world. From the dark 'time tunnel', they had emerged into the colour, noise and smells of a lively Viking settlement. Groups of model figures peopled the reconstructed dwellings, worked in workshops, set foot on boats. Mike was delighted.

'But they are not real!' exclaimed Pascal.

'Of course not,' grinned Mike.

'Not even holograms?' Pascal looked puzzled. 'But we travelled back.'

Mike stopped grinning.

'We pretended to.'

'Ah, I see. You only have models, then. Can I touch them?'

'No, I shouldn't do that. Look, Pascal, you don't have real, live models in French museums, do you? What exactly do you mean?'

Pascal paused.

'How silly of me,' he said carefully. 'I meant . . . I thought they looked so realistic. I thought they were real.' He began looking very attentively at the exhibits.

'This way, everyone,' called Mr Rossiter. 'Into the education room.'

An enthusiastic young man got to work on them. Mike noticed that Pascal understood everything that was said. He had taken this for granted up to now, but comparing him with the other French students, he realized just how advanced he was. He even stayed behind to ask questions.

'Don't be down-hearted,' said a voice in Mike's ear. Mr Dewsbury stood there. 'He's unusually fluent. Don't expect you can quite match that.'

'Can't at all, Sir.'

'Neither could I, at that age. Can't quite place his accent, though. I'll have to ask him where he comes from. Go and get him. Mustn't keep the Mayor waiting.'

On their return home, both Mike and Pascal declined Mum's offer of a meal on the grounds that the Mayor had given them a good tea. 'I'll not keep you from the cakes,' he had said, making a very short speech, and Mike had felt he was a sensible sort of man. Liz had played a couple of board games with them but Pascal had gone to bed early. Mike had followed soon after, and, taking out his diary, he tried to express his conflicting feelings.

'I must be going mad,' he wrote. 'Something is going on, I'm sure, but what? I am all at sea.' He was quite pleased with this image. 'I seem to have slipped my anchor and am drifting towards the rocks. floating helplessly; I am pounded by waves of confusion and doubt.' He stopped, irritated. Why did he always get more involved in the writing than the reality? Usually, of course, because it was the most interesting part, but that was not true this time. The reality was so bewildering, he was trying to escape from it. He decided to be practical. He would list the important factors.

1. Something strange happened with Bazzer and Gav.

2. Pascal is not an ordinary French school kid. Now I've seen all the others, I realize they are like Liz and me. Pascal is different.

3. Pascal can read thoughts.

He rubbed that out, then wrote it again. He felt it was true.

4. In the museum, he thought we were really going back in time. I'm sure he did.

5. And what about the coach?

That was really strange, he thought. Pascal not only failed to notice that it was a French make, he did not know how it worked. Where in France didn't they know about coach travel? It was daft. He read his list again but did not know what to make of it. He made a decision.

'Tomorrow, I shall speak to Liz about this.'

He snapped the diary shut. He had decided. He put off the light. But he just kept thinking of the day's events. He thought of Fraser. He seemed very carefree. He thought of the discussion group. He smiled wryly as he thought of Mrs Wagstaffe's praise for their 'joint' effort. Pascal had stepped in and saved him there.

As Mike thought about him, Pascal was concluding his nightly contact with the Seniors. They had been interested in the whole day and did not share Pascal's anxieties.

'You are unnecessarily disturbed,' the Senior was saying. 'The boy is uneasy, but he is alone in this and his thoughts are confused.'

'I don't want to be unfair to Mike.'

'Unfair? You have no agreement with him.'

'It is an unspoken agreement. It is friendship.'

There was a pause.

'You occupy your mind with trivialities. You will not harm him. There is no need to think in this way. Tune in to the boy. He is not hostile towards you.'

At that moment, remembering the group discussion, and wanting to be scrupulously fair, Mike put on the light, picked up his diary again, and wrote,

'Despite everything, I would like Pascal to be my friend.'

Chapter Six

MIKE SLEPT BADLY and rose early. He knew he was in
a bad way when he went down the garden and cleaned
out the rabbits. It usually took a full range of reminders
from Mum, from hint to ultimatum, before he got
round to it. Grandad kept rabbits, too. Mike thought of
him and suddenly he very much wanted to go and see
him. He felt he must have a rest from the turmoil in his
head.

'You're up early,' said Mum as he came through the
back door. 'Want some breakfast? Dad and I are going
out for the day so we want to make an early start.'

'I'll wait and get breakfast for the others,' said Mike.

'Don't worry, I'll be back in time to do a proper dinner tonight,' she promised. 'I'm not deserting you.'

'Thought we'd go over and see Grandad today.'

'Oh yes, do that,' nodded Mum. 'I was talking to him
yesterday and he's got some photographs of France he'd
like to show Pascal.'

Mum and Dad had gone before the others came down.
Liz was in a lively mood and said Pascal ought to get the
breakfast. She could not believe, she insisted, that he did
not know how to make toast. She showed him how and
he tried it with honey, marmalade and jam. Mike
advised against the brown sauce. Liz imagined that
Pascal must come from a very formal home where
everything was just so. He had obviously never done

anything like this before though he did seem to be thoroughly enjoying himself. She looked at Mike. He was watching Pascal and she thought he seemed tense.

They walked over to Grandad's where they had a mug of tea and got bogged down in a discussion about the difference between a mug and a cup. This seemed to fascinate Pascal.

'It's only the difference between the shape of the container,' said Mike.

'Oh no!' said Liz firmly. 'It's not just that, it's a *statement*. A mug says, "Relax, we don't stand on ceremony here". When we go to our games teacher's flat after a match, it says, "I'm one of you, really". When our history teacher offers us mugs, it's saying, "I have working-class roots, don't forget". Mum likes us to use proper cups and saucers because she can still remember what it's like to be poor.'

Mike gaped. He was learning a lot about his family since Pascal had come. Grandad was smiling.

'Quite right,' he nodded. 'My statement is "I hate washing up".'

Liz grinned. 'We'll do it while you and Pascal look at the photos.'

As they washed up, they looked out of the window at Grandad and Pascal sitting on a seat in the little garden, surrounded by photograph albums.

'We should take more interest,' said Liz suddenly. 'That's real history.'

'Pascal likes all this, doesn't he?' said Mike. 'He wants to learn all the time. About everything.' He hesitated and dried a spoon carefully.

'Well, I've got it all worked out,' said Liz confidently.

'I would guess that his parents are quite old. He's a late child.' Liz pulled out the plug with a dramatic gesture. 'Pascal is very clever so they encourage him.' She, could now see the grey-haired couple beaming fondly on their gifted offspring. 'He sits in his own study, working so much that he doesn't get out and mix with people his own age.'

'He is sort of old-fashioned and serious,' admitted Mike, 'but it's more than that. Would you think I was crazy if I said that sometimes I feel that he can read my thoughts? The other day, when I asked what he normally did, he used the same phrase I was thinking of at that very moment.'

'But he's very sensitive,' Liz argued, but she paused. She was thinking of the cinema. A touch and a look and he had understood her. He was incredibly sensitive. 'I know what you mean though.'

Mike took the plunge. 'Something happened after the barn dance. For some reason, Bazzer and Gav have got it in for us.'

'But they're idiots,' Liz said indignantly.

'Yes, but tough idiots. It's almost as if they want to punish me for being friends with a foreigner.'

'Yes,' said Liz, 'that sounds like that lovely human being, our Bazzer. I sometimes feel sorry for Gav, and anyway, he'd make a salted peanut look intelligent. But Bazzer! There's something really creepy about Bazzer. He *needs* to be nasty.'

'I knew he was on the look out for us and, of course, we walked right into them after the dance.'

Liz put the scouring powder down carefully. 'What happened?' she asked.

'Well, that's the problem. I'm not sure. Bazzer was going to attack us, I'm sure of that, and Pascal just raised his arm and stopped him.'

'What do you mean? How?'

'Bazzer and Gav just collided with each other and Pascal and I ran for it.'

'They misjudged it. They bumped into each other.'

'It wasn't like that.' Mike knew it all sounded a bit unlikely. 'They'd planned it. Bazzer had brought a spray can of paint.'

'What!' Liz all but exploded. 'Bazzer ought to be locked up,' she declared indignantly.

'I know it sounds stupid, but I'm sure that when Pascal threw up his arm, he made them crash into each other. I know he didn't touch them.'

Liz pulled a face. 'It all sounds a bit odd,' she said, 'but I don't like all this about Bazzer. Do we say anything to Dad?'

'That wouldn't help.' Mike could see that Liz was distracted by the obvious awfulness of Bazzer. That, she could believe. 'Anyway, we can't say anything to Dad about Pascal reading minds.'

Liz came to a decision. 'Look, we'll have to have it out with Pascal. We'll tell him we don't understand what is going on and ask for some explanations.'

They looked out of the window. Grandad and Pascal had moved over to the rabbit hutches and Grandad was giving Pascal the big white doe to hold. When Liz and Mike went outside, Pascal was transformed. His eyes were shining and he was stroking the rabbit.

'I have great admiration for this texture,' he was saying softly, 'and beneath, I feel the life of the creature. And it seems to trust me!'

'Haven't you got a pet of your own, lad?' asked Grandad.

'I am afraid not. Where I live, there are no creatures like this, and no grass for them.'

'City lad, eh?' said Grandad, sympathetically.

'Yes, a city,' agreed Pascal. Liz and Mike looked at each other. Pascal seldom volunteered information about his home. 'Streets, whiteness, hard textures.' He stroked the rabbit's fur. 'Many people living together. There has to be order, you see, or the system would break down.' He sighed. 'Pets would be a problem.'

'There's only one thing for it, then,' Grandad said heartily. 'You'll have to come over every year and visit us. The next time we have young rabbits, you can choose one and it can be yours.' And Grandad took a photograph of Pascal holding the rabbit.

As he handed the rabbit back, he smiled at Mike. Mike met his eyes and gazed steadily. For a moment, Mike saw a change in Pascal's expression and knew they understood each other. He had to ask Pascal some questions and it seemed that Pascal would not be unprepared for them.

But Grandad's house was a haven; neutral ground, and they passed the rest of the day in watchful quiet. They enjoyed beans and yet more toast, then helped Grandad to clear out his shed, just as Liz and Mike used to when they were little and Mum had gone out for the day. Pascal seemed to be at peace, too. When it was time to go, he shook hands with Grandad and went out once more to stroke the rabbit.

Liz whispered to Mike. 'Tonight,' she said, 'after we've eaten. We'll try to get to the bottom of this. We'll set up a game of Dungeons and Dragons. That will get rid of Mum and Dad. Then we'll tackle him.'

'OK,' agreed Mike, 'but whatever we think, honestly, it can't be anything really bad. Can it?'

In fact, there were no Dungeons and Dragons that night. Mum and Dad were already back and particularly cheerful. They had been planning the rest of the holidays and had decided on a series of family outings for Pascal's benefit. There was an historic event tomorrow, a visit to London one day, a stately home another. Dad was planning to book them all into a Shakespeare play on an evening when he had to do something else and Pascal had delighted everyone else by saying,

'No, really, Mr Castle, Shakespeare is very good indeed. You should give him a try.'

'Pascal saw right through you!' crowed Mum triumphantly, and Mike and Liz exchanged glances.

'Now for a good dinner,' announced Mum. 'Something special tonight. I'm mixing and matching from my new cookery books,' she explained to Pascal.

'Is that wise?' asked Liz.

'Now, now,' said Dad. 'I've been helping. It's going to be an occasion.'

'Our food is a bit boring,' declared Mrs Castle, bustling between the refrigerator and the cooker. 'Not like French cuisine, Pascal. I love French food shops. They always make everything look as nice as it tastes.'

'Pascal doesn't mind ordinary English food.' Mike was making one last attempt to protect their guest from his mother's cooking but it was far too late. Mrs Castle intended to dazzle them.

They started with a thin, pale-green soup which was

not too bad, nor too good, for that matter. Mike avoided asking what it was made of. They all waited for Mrs Castle to take the first spoonful and, as she seemed all right, they followed. The second course was more a feast for the eye. It was to be Fish Surprise *Flambé*. A sea of chopped, savoury jelly, rather a bright green, supported an intricate fishing-net made of criss-crossed, thin chips which had clearly taken a long time to arrange. Balanced on top were whole fish. As their heads were still on, they glared around the table, giving a distinctly nasty look to anyone brave enough to meet their eyes. The triumph of the dish, however, apparently lay in the sauce which contained brandy, and Mrs Castle was going to set light to it.

'It never works properly with the Christmas pudding,' cautioned Liz.

'Yes, but that's because your Dad just guesses how to do it,' Mrs Castle replied confidently. 'This is from a recipe, written by an expert.'

It might well have been written by the SAS. A sheet of flame briefly but dramatically lit up the room. Black flakes of fish drifted down over the fused chips which now resembled a well-tarred lobster pot, and melting green jelly oozed across the cloth. There was a silence, and then the doorbell rang.

Liz stood up, wiped a few, stray black flakes from her face and said, 'I'll go' in a voice of quiet, heroic calm.

The spell broke when she opened the door. A rather tall, tanned, very blond boy of about her own age stood on the step. He smiled in a way that made Liz clutch the door handle.

'I must apologize,' he said. 'I realize now, I should

have telephoned.'

He spoke excellent English but there was a definite accent. It reminded Liz of the French film stars she'd seen on television in old Hollywood musicals.

'I am so late,' he continued. 'You must have thought I would not come. I am your exchange student, Pascal Monet.'

Chapter Seven

EVEN MIKE was filled with admiration for his parents. The affair of the exploding fish heads, followed by the arrival of a guest on their very doorstep brought out the Dunkirk spirit in them both. Dad said whatever the muddle was, they were going to have some supper first and shot off to the fish and chip shop. Not renowned for his tact, he nevertheless thought again, crossed the road and went to the Chinese take-away. By the time he came back, Mum had organized a human chain from the airing cupboard to a camp-bed in the dining room, which the newcomer declared ideal. Seated around the table again, they checked the papers he had received from the Exchange Agency. They stated quite clearly that Pascal Nicolas Monet was destined for the Castle family at Number 17 Worcester Way.

'It's the Agency's fault,' declared Dad. 'After all, they handed over little Pascal themselves. It will be because of you two having the same name.'

'You must call me Nik or we will be in confusion, too!' Nik smiled. Liz thought of Coca Cola advertisements.

'I was very slightly ill, but it was all nonsense. It passed very quickly and I thought "I can make this journey myself, by air. Why not?" But I am so stupid. I should have telephoned.'

'No, no,' insisted Mum. 'Don't give it another

thought. It's only for a few days, after all. It's been love-ly having Pascal and we shall enjoy having you here as well. We've even got some outings lined up. The more the merrier!'

Mike looked at Liz. He needed to talk to her. Liz was looking at Nik. She wasn't thinking clearly. She didn't realize that Nik's obviously genuine appearance confirmed their suspicions. Pascal was very quiet. Mike noticed that when Nik spoke to him, he answered in English. From time to time, he closed his eyes, head back and nodded a little.

'We'll leave you young people to make some plans,' said Mum, 'but don't stay up too long, Pascal. You look tired and we've a long day tomorrow.'

Mike and Liz cleared the table while Nik chatted to Pascal. In the hall, Mike grabbed Liz's arm but she was hardly listening.

'Things are looking up!' said Liz. 'I think I'm going to have to phone my friends and make them all jealous.'

'But don't you see!' Mike was getting desperate. 'If Nik's the real exchange, who is Pascal?'

'Oh Mike,' said Liz loftily, 'grow up! It was an Agency mistake. You were there. That woman handed Pascal over. OK, he's a very sensitive lad. But no more than that. You wouldn't recognize a sensitive soul if he hit you with a pickaxe handle.'

She swept back into the dining room. Nik stood up as she entered.

After that, Mike and Pascal said very little but their silence was not noticed.

'Your mother was right,' Pascal said at last. 'I am very tired. I shall go to bed.'

'Oh, right,' said Mike. 'Think I'll go up, too.' Everyone stood up. Everyone shook hands.

'*A demain!*' said Nik.

'Oh, right,' said Mike again. '*Dormez bien.*' He trudged up the stairs behind Pascal. Exploding fish, shaking hands, speaking French. He wondered how long he could go on.

Once in bed, he reached automatically for his diary. He licked his pencil then wished he had not.

'Shall I get lead poisoning?' he wrote. Strange how strong the instinct for self-preservation was. 'No, they are not made of lead anymore. I am very worried.' He rubbed that out. He must not allow his mind to wander. He must try to set everything out clearly. 'This morning, I told Liz about Pascal. I know she felt something was up, too. He is not an ordinary person. His mind works differently. And everything is new to him. I know he's French, but . . .' Mike stopped. He realized that he did not know that. It was suddenly clear to him that it was not English things that were new to him, it was ordinary things. Things you would find almost anywhere. Mike's stomach began to churn. He was getting carried away. He thought quickly of the visit to Grandad. 'Whatever he is, he is not bad. I'm sure of that. He loved the rabbit.' Mike asked himself why that should be so reassuring. Then he wrote, 'He respects life.' He sighed and began to relax a little. He started to write again.

'I sometimes wonder if Mum does. Her cooking will bring me to an early grave.' His tired brain rested on a picture of a little grave, marked by a simple headstone. He could see a short but dignified inscription on it: 'Michael Castle. It was the meringue. RIP'. His thoughts came back to Liz. Before, she had believed him, but now

Nik had come, she was only interested in him. Mike did not really blame her – Nik was tall, blond and handsome, he supposed. He returned to his diary: 'I bet everyone else in my class has got an ordinary French boy who plays football and collects records. Why me? I've got two of them. One of them is really sophisticated and the other is . . .' Mike lay back and closed his eyes. Yes, that was the problem. What?

At that moment he heard Pascal call out to him. He sat up and threw back the covers. Then he realized that the house was silent. The voice was in his head.

When Pascal closed his bedroom door behind him, he did not bother to undress. He was pressing lightly on the bronze link even before he sat down. The screen came to life immediately but with none of the force of the previous transmission. The response was quick but soothing. A different Senior appeared, one who had trained Pascal.

'There are unsuspected complexities, Young One. You are well?'

'I am well but unsure of my path now.'

'Of course. We have been careless. We have made assumptions. You are not to blame. We have decided to withdraw from this mission and undertake more research. We see now that we have been premature.'

'But I cannot return at once. I cannot just disappear. The family would be distressed.'

'Yes,' said the Senior, thoughtfully, 'we have noticed this concern you have developed. But you need not worry yourself,' he continued briskly. 'Any discomfort of mind among the humans can be eradicated.'

'No,' said Pascal, 'not Mike.'

'What do you mean? Elucidate.'

'Mike is very disturbed in his mind. He realizes that I am different. I need the power to make him understand.'

'You endanger yourself. Your thinking becomes unprocessed.'

'I will take the risk,' said Pascal. It was the first time he had ever opposed a Senior. 'I do not believe Mike will betray me and I owe it to him. He has become my friend.'

'A friend?' asked the Senior. 'Indeed? Most interesting.' There was a long pause while Pascal and the Senior faced each other, gazing intently. 'It shall be done.' The Senior had decided. 'You will complete this short visit and you will return as simply as you came. That can all be arranged. Who would believe this boy, after all? Yes, it shall be done.'

Pascal, satisfied and happy, waited for the screen to fade.

'One moment. I would like you to monitor the woman, tomorrow. We had understood that burnt offerings and similar sacrifices disappeared many centuries ago. The fascinating re-creation of an underwater scene, followed by sacrifice by fire, must refer to worship of the elements. She buried the remnants in the garden. Thus, we have earth, fire and water. I anticipate a ritual associated with air. Please transmit carefully when it occurs.

The room returned to normal.

'I have changed,' Pascal thought to himself. 'I have made a decision and I know that the Seniors do not understand about Mrs Castle's food preparations. But I do, and I am . . .' He was obliged to speak aloud in one of the languages of Earth '. . . amused!'

Turning the door handle softly, Mike peeped round and was surprised to see Pascal sitting cross-legged on his bed, looking lively and smiling broadly.

'Mike,' he said, 'come in. I have something to say to you. Something difficult to believe but I think you begin to understand already. But after that,' he continued urgently, 'I want you to explain to me about jokes.'

'Sorry to disturb you again,' Mike wrote in his diary. 'This has been a weird evening. Have talked with Pascal for hours. I was right. He is not French. The chain he wears is a transmitter. He let me wear it and I knew everything he said was true. He can't stay, though. He's going back at the end of the exchange. I asked him about Bazzer and Gav and I was right about that, too. He says he's not allowed to interfere anymore so we've still got that problem. My problem, I suppose. I'll still be here when everyone has gone back. There was one thing Pascal said that I liked. He didn't have to tell me everything, but he wanted to. He said it was because he is my friend.'

Mike read over what he had just written. Then, quite deliberately, he began to rub the whole thing out. He'd have to go back and do a bit of editing. He felt perfectly satisfied. He slept well.

Chapter Eight

MIKE overslept the next morning. He awoke very suddenly, hearing Dad's voice at close range. He was standing by Mike's bed, holding a tray and bellowing, '*Je t'adore.*'

'What?' asked Mike weakly, struggling to sit up.

'That means "I see you are still asleep".'

'No, Dad, it doesn't,' Mike told him, subsiding again.

'Well, get this down you and get up. Have you forgotten what day it is?'

Mike looked at him and remembered. 'The battle!' he said. 'I'd forgotten all about the battle!'

'Thought you had,' said Dad complacently. He lowered his voice. 'Brought you some toast as well. Told your mother you looked tired and needed breakfast in bed.'

Mike was amazed. 'Breakfast in bed! She'd be suspicious at once.'

'She may not have entirely grasped what I was saying,' said Dad, as he left the room. 'I told her in French.'

When Mike walked into the kitchen, it was hard to decide who was the more astonished at his appearance, Pascal or Nik.

'But what is this? This is the costume of long ago!'

Mike was wearing a leather, sleeveless coat over baggy trousers which reached his knees. A broad white collar to his shirt and long white socks gave him a rather demure air but he was also wearing a sword. Before Mike could answer, Mr Castle entered. His buff

66

coat seemed to cover several acres and his large collar made him quite cherubic. He swept off a broad-brimmed hat and bowed.

'At your service, gentlemen. Are you for the King or Parliament?'

'This I like,' grinned Nik. 'Permit me to try your hat?'

'*Certainement*,' said Dad. 'Try this helmet, too.'

'But what is happening?' asked Pascal. 'We are still in the same time band, are we not?'

'No wonder you're confused,' said Mrs Castle. 'It's an association, a leisure time activity.' She thought Pascal looked quite anxious. 'It's for people interested in the English Civil War. They re-enact events from that time and wear authentic clothes.'

'Actually,' said Liz, 'they do a lot of good work for charities as well. Today, they are re-enacting the Battle of Naseby and raising money for a children's hospital.'

'I see,' said Nik. 'It is some history and some spectacle, like an historical play.'

'It is history with action,' declared Mike with enthusiasm.

'And a bit of dressing up,' added Mum, looking at her husband adjusting his cloak.

'Vain as a peacock,' said Liz.

'Kindly do not mention peacocks in front of your mother,' said Mr Castle loftily. 'She is quite capable of giving us one for dinner.'

'With blazing tail feathers,' said Pascal eagerly.

Everyone looked at him in surprise and then laughed.

'Good for you, Pascal,' said Mum. 'You're getting the idea. Come and help me to make these salads. We'll be out all day.'

Mike always wished they could travel to the Historic Battle Society's meetings on horseback. There was something uncomfortable about putting the pikes on the roof-rack, Dad's big hat on the parcel shelf and seeing him wearing his fancy collar behind the wheel. He felt it impaired the judgement of other drivers at traffic lights. They had left many a stalled vehicle as the drivers gaped into their car, fumbling for the wrong gear. They drove out of town and into the lanes.

'It is green, green, green,' said Pascal dreamily.

'You come from the South?' asked Nik.

'I come from where it is not green,' Pascal replied.

'I'll tell you something about the battle,' Mike said quickly. 'There's quite a lot of us — several regiments. Some are Royalists, some Parliamentarians. Where we're going is very near to the original battle site so it will be a re-enactment over the same sort of ground.'

'I'm with the pikes, Mike's with the cannons,' added Dad.

'I shall see a cannon? Working?' asked Pascal, his eyes wide.

'And hear one!' said Liz.

'But who was fighting?' persisted Pascal.

'The King's army, led by Prince Rupert, and the New Model Army, led by one of Cromwell's most famous commanders, Fairfax. It was 1645, the last decisive battle, really, of the Civil War.'

'But why did they not talk?'

'They had talked. They'd been talking for a long time; but in the end, it was war.

Pascal shook his head.

'Don't worry,' said Mum. 'People are very stupid

sometimes, but we are improving.'

'You believe that?' asked Nik. 'Truly?'

'Yes,' said Mum firmly, 'and you're all part of it. Your Europe will be different from ours. More of a family and that must be good. After all, you get cross with the family but you don't bomb them.'

'Hah!' said Liz. 'What about the Fish Surprise?'

'You know what I mean! It's all up to you young people. We're relying on you.'

'If you want to enjoy this, Pascal,' said Mike, returning to the immediate problem, 'you had better think of it as an all-action play, but it will be as near to the truth as we can get it.'

Nik looked out of the window and yelped. A motor cyclist, conventionally clad in a crash helmet, overtook at speed. Rather less conventionally, he was also wearing a large white collar with many fine points of lace fluttering in the breeze.

'Bloomin' cavalry,' grumbled Dad. 'Trust a Cavalier to cut you up.'

'You are a Republican, like me, Mr Castle,' laughed Nik.

'Today, I am for the people, the ordinary, simple folk.'

'Well, that's definitely you, dear,' observed Mrs Castle.

A Volvo swept by, more pikes on the roof-rack and a plumed hat in the back. Then they overtook a struggling car, advanced in years, pulling a trailer. The Castles all waved and cheered. 'Our cannon,' explained Mike.

Soon, every vehicle they saw presented a picture of past and present co-existing in cheerful confusion. Pascal was almost disorientated, but Nik sensed a party atmosphere.

'If I had known, I would have dressed up, too, but I would be a Cavalier.'

'Inconsistent!' complained Mum. 'first you chop off your king's head, then you want to be a Cavalier.'

'Yes, Mum,' said Liz, 'but we did, too. That's why we're here today.'

'Oh yes,' said Mum, laughing at herself. 'Of course we did. You French,' she amended her remark, 'are as inconsistent as the British.'

They turned off, into a large field. Tents had been set up and there were market stalls on one side and a very wide roped-off enclosure beyond them. It was a sloping site, topped by a spinney of trees and with a long hedge running down one side. They stopped at the entrance and Mr Castle was checked in.

'It's good fun, but the organizers are quite careful about everything because of the weapons and gunpowder.'

They parked the car and Mr Castle and Mike unloaded their equipment and went to report for duty.

'We'll have lunch,' said Mrs Castle. 'It's a bit early but we can then find good places to watch the battle from. The general public will start coming in soon.' Pascal still looked anxious.

'They will really fight then?'

Liz smiled at him.

'Now don't worry,' she said. 'It's a mock battle. They'll just give us a picture of what happened on this day in 1645. It's quite important, you see. From that day, things could never be quite the same again. The monarchy was restored but kings and queens never again had the same power over the people.'

'This is your democracy?' asked Pascal.

Liz sighed.

'Well, yes, but it's not really that simple.'

'In my opinion,' said Mrs Castle firmly, 'this is a good excuse for all those males to have a good fight.'

'You could be right,' Liz grinned, 'though some of them are female. At least it's constructive. It's organized and the charities benefit.'

'You mean,' Pascal looked quite pale, 'they still have these primitive instincts? They want to hurt each other?'

Liz sighed again.

'Pascal,' she said, 'with you, it's never the easy answer, is it? Most of them don't actually want to hurt anyone but they still seem to like fighting.'

'Some of them actually like history,' said Mrs Castle, determined to be fair.

'The people here aren't like Bazzer and Gav,' added Liz.

'Not like Bazzer and Gav,' murmured Pascal. 'They do not fight for a noble cause.'

'You can say that again,' said Liz warmly and would have enlarged on what she felt about Bazzer and Gav, but Pascal followed her instruction to say it again and she had to explain English figures of speech, a process which delighted Nik but confused Pascal who seemed to think that you should always say exactly what you meant.

Mr Castle returned with Mike and they started their picnic.

'When you come to France, and you must all come,' Nik said expansively, 'I will take you on a French picnic. The river is very low in the summer and we take bread and cheese and perhaps wine, down to the river bed. There is corner in the river —'

'A bend,' corrected Mrs Castle absently. 'Yes?'

'A bend in the river where the trees hang over. We sit on the hot stones but have shade for our heads.'

'Perfect,' sighed Mrs Castle. 'It can be lovely here but the weather is so unreliable.'

'But it changes,' said Pascal. 'I like that.'

Nik looked at him curiously.

'Well, yes, I suppose the temperature is more consistent in the South.'

But Pascal was not really listening.

'Always suitable, always the same,' he was murmuring, almost to himself. 'I prefer change.'

'Well,' said Mike rather loudly, 'shall we go and look at the market stalls? We've got about half an hour before we have to be in place.'

'Yoo hoo!' trilled a voice. 'All the Castles together. How nice!' A woman fluttered about in front of them, examining Pascal and Nik very closely. Liz had leaped to her feet.

'Hello, Mrs York,' she said. 'Just off to see the sights,' and the boys found themselves propelled away at speed.

'Two French guests?' asked Mrs York. This was a piece of information she had known nothing about. Her extensive intelligence network had failed her.

'Certainement,' said Dad. 'Doing our best for the European Communauté.'

'Oh, Mr Castle!' shrieked Mrs York, 'you're speaking French!'

'Really?' said Mum.

'Of course,' the woman continued, 'I could tell the little dark-haired one was French. You can always tell, can't you? The tall, blond one doesn't look right. Perhaps he's an Alsatian.'

72

'No,' said Dad, 'he's definitely French and human.'

Mrs York shrieked again.

'Mr Castle! You are dreadful! Do they cost a lot to feed?'

'Alsatians?' asked Dad. 'Cost a fortune, I believe.'

'No difficulties at all, Mrs York,' said Mum shortly. 'They're just a couple of nice lads. Individuals like anyone else.'

'Of course they are,' Mrs York agreed warmly. 'I think you're wonderful to take them on, I really do.'

'Let battle commence,' said Dad, standing up suddenly. 'Action stations. To your post, Mrs York.'

'Oh, Mr Castle,' gasped Mrs York and scuttled off.

Dad sat down again.

'Still another twenty minutes. Fancy another cup of tea?'

'You are dreadful, Mr Castle,' said Mum, accepting the cup. 'Still, I do find that woman pretty hard to take.'

'She lives in a very small world,' observed Dad. 'Trouble is, she thinks it's the only one.'

'Our two won't be like that,' said Mum confidently. 'I think they're starting right.'

'You really believe in this international exchange business, don't you?'

'My father didn't come back from the war,' said Mum briefly.

Dad nodded and stood up again.

'And here we are, celebrating another battle.'

'Remembering,' said Mum.

Dad waved.

'That's Mike,' he said. 'The others are coming over. Get yourselves good seats. It will be a bit of English history for our guests. See you later.'

Chapter Nine

MRS CASTLE produced four bars of chocolate and passed them along the line. Nik alternately bit into his and waved it in the air as he interrogated Liz about the battle site. Mrs Castle thought Pascal still looked rather troubled as he carefully broke his chocolate into small squares and ate them silently.

Soon, they heard a distant beat of drums and they all looked across to the far side of the arena. Lines of men were moving into position to a slow, measured beat. The cannons were dragged into position and they could just distinguish Mike from the others. Liz was astonished, as ever, by the colours – red, blue, green.

'Fancy going into battle in a scarlet coat with blue facings and rows of shining buttons,' sighed Liz. 'It all seems so absurd.'

'The trouble is,' said Mum ruefully, 'it all looks wonderful, doesn't it?'

There was a stir a little further along as a group of people, even more colourfully dressed than the armies, began to move around the enclosure.

'Look who's coming,' smiled Mrs Castle, cheering up.

Cheers and laughter broke out and some of the crowd started waving, and were graciously acknowledged by the processing group.

'It's His Majesty,' said Liz. 'Here's your chance to see Charles the First!'

'Wearing his head,' added Nik. He was loving it.

Pascal looked in astonishment as the group of courtiers approached. He looked so bewildered that Liz said, 'They're actors,' and then felt rather silly for stating the obvious. They were richly dressed and wearing flowing wigs. The King carried a gold-topped stick, and raised his lace-fringed hand elegantly, if languidly, to respond to the cheers of his loyal subjects, most of whom were dressed in jeans and T-shirts. Liz smiled.

'Very good,' she conceded. 'See his long, thin face? He looks just like the Van Dyck portrait.'

'Bravo!' cried Nik, applauding loudly and he was rewarded by a gracious wave from a king on the edge of the end of his life.

As the group passed, they were followed by a less elegant mob who cheeked the crowd and threw apples. They were the camp followers, the people who followed the coat-tails of an army, existing as best they could. Pascal was staring at one character who was cleverly made up as a beggar, his face hideous with filth and sores. Liz and Mrs Castle knew him. Normally he was a butcher who kept an impeccably clean shop and called all his customers 'madam'. A jaunty little dog, thoroughly enjoying itself, ran beside and around him. Pascal became rigid as the beggar lunged at Liz, calling her 'my angel' and demanding money.

'Unhand her, you monster,' cried an imperious voice. Mrs York, in a girlishly flowing wig and an approximation of a seventeenth-century gown, swept up.

'It's all right,' said Liz and gave him a coin.

'Don't give him anything,' said Mrs York. 'He'll only buy drink.'

'Isn't that more nineteenth century?' objected the beggar, but Mrs York wrested the coin from him and put it in her own basket.

The little dog, who loved the butcher, was incensed and grabbed Mrs York's hem and began to worry it, growling fiercely. The other rag-tag citizens rushed to the rescue and the mob moved on looking like a very authentic rabble.

'She is the most interfering busybody I know!' spluttered Mrs Castle, further words failing her.

'There's Mike,' said Liz, pointing to a knot of soldiers gathered round a cannon.

'But will he be harmed?' Pascal was finding the whole experience full of unaccustomed anxieties.

'Now look, don't worry,' said Liz. 'He's been trained. Most of it's planned, and it's not real, after all.'

'No, it's not real, is it?' Pascal seemed to be trying to understand, without much success.

'That's the king's army over there,' explained Liz. 'His men are on two grass ridges with a dip between them, just as they were in 1645. Prince Rupert started it all off. He led his cavalry down the slope and the king's foot-soldiers followed it through. The Parliamentary forces were shaken but Cromwell was right over there with a larger number of horsemen and, in the end, the king's men were out-numbered. You'll see the cavalry come down in a minute, then the infantry will come forward. It will be a bit of a scrum in the middle but watch the edge of the arena as well. The actors will be staging little incidents.'

'It looks very good,' said Nik approvingly. He pointed to the top of the hill where the king was now seated

76

on a horse and banners were flying bravely. The noise built up, the shouting and drumming grew louder.

Mrs Castle glanced at Pascal's face and wondered if they ought to have brought him. He seemed so tense and bewildered. She began to wonder if his family had suffered some dreadful wartime experience. They had very easily assumed that everyone would see it as an interesting historical reconstruction, not anything like a real battle. Then she saw his head lift and his eyes widen. He gave a little gasp. He was gazing at the Royalist horsemen as they swept across the arena, showing off for the crowd.

'Actually,' said Liz, eyeing the pounding hoofs and flying plumes with a critical expression, 'in the real battle, half of them made off after the first encounter, leaving the infantry with no cover on the left wing.'

But Pascal was following the horses with all his attention, drinking in the sight.

'Are you fond of horses, Pascal?' asked Mrs Castle kindly, feeling very relieved at the change.

'I think I am,' he answered with a little smile.

For Pascal, the rest of the battle was a picture of horses galloping, wheeling and side-stepping, manes and tails flying. The others alternately watched the skirmishes in midfield and the scenes enacted round the perimeter. They could see Mr Castle's group edging out, gradually coming nearer. Mike was only occasionally visible but they heard the reports and saw the smoke rising above the struggle. From a distance, it looked formidable but as Mr Castle approached, snatches of conversation reached them that suggested that most people were enjoying themselves.

'Watch where you're putting that thing. I'm on your side,' cried a perspiring officer.

'Sorry, mate,' and the pair were lost to view again as the armies clashed, surging back towards the centre.

They turned their attention to the actors. A preacher made a last effort to save souls, women looked for their husbands. A seventeenth-century cart trundled by as help was brought to the 'wounded'. They caught sight of Mrs York again. She rushed to the fallen with a water bottle and they saw her tread on a man's hand and spill water over him in one swift movement.

'Don't ask me to translate that,' said Liz as the man sat up, protesting loudly.

'I guess it,' said Nik, grinning. He was watching everything with keen attention and asked questions all the time. An interesting thought struck him.

'What will happen if, this time, the Royalists win?'

'You must prevent it,' said Pascal immediately. 'Deviations are dangerous.'

'Don't worry about that,' said Mum. 'The others will get their own back next time.'

Pascal sat down suddenly as if it was all too much. 'Come on, lads, to me! To me!' Mr Castle's voice could be heard clearly now, and suddenly, they burst out of the scrum and threw themselves to the ground, puffing mightily.

'Oh dear,' said Mum. 'I'm afraid Mrs York has spotted them. She's going to minister to them.'

Mrs York came pounding over, calling to the other camp followers to help her. She was making a big production of attending to the fallen. They heard Dad being polite.

'Don't bother, Mrs York,' he was saying. 'We've just come over for a little rest until we're needed.'

'You poor, poor men,' shrilled Mrs York.

'No really,' said Dad, 'we're just having a breather.' He got up awkwardly.

'I will bathe your brow,' she insisted. Mrs York was very determined. 'Sit here and rest.' For a moment it looked as if she might bring Mr Castle down with a rugby tackle. She rolled up her sleeves.

'Wait for it,' said Liz, as a look of extreme irritation crossed Dad's face.

'Who are you, woman?' he suddenly bellowed. 'A spy. A spy, my friends. This woman is a Royalist spy!'

Two actors rushed over and seized her by the arms. Mrs York was delighted.

'I am loyal to Cromwell and the people,' she screamed as they dragged her away. 'I was at the siege of Oxford.'

'Didn't get to Oxford,' commented one of the soldiers, still lying on the grass on one elbow and fanning himself with his hat. 'Our bus broke down.'

A red-faced messenger panted up. 'Come on,' he shouted. 'You're wanted. It's our turn.'

'Pascal, your face is a picture,' said Mrs Castle. 'Come and sit by me and I'll try and explain.'

The players round the edge of the arena gradually left and a charge from the Parliamentarians began the final set of manoeuvres which were to decide the fate of England. They watched the advances and retreats. Nik chattered enthusiastically, his English breaking down from time to time in his excitement. Pascal kept his eyes on the distant action where he could see the bright, brave colours and admire the flying pennants as the horses galloped across the ridge.

When it was over and they had applauded the armies as they circled the arena for the last time, they returned to the car. Dad and Mike joined them and they presented an interesting sight. Dad's helmet had been trodden on by a horse and Mike's broad, white collar was now a broad, black collar. They were both well pleased with their day. As they drove home, Nik questioned them closely about the movements of the battle and they explained how they had tried to reproduce the original battle plan. Mrs Castle saw Pascal relax as their cheerful chat revealed a complex game rather than any form of warfare.

'Let's stop for fish and chips,' suggested Mike as they reached the outskirts of the town. 'Mum won't want to cook tonight.'

Dad took Nik and Pascal off to buy supper as he said going to the fish and chip shop was an essential British experience. He seemed oblivious of his unusual appearance.

'Poor Pascal,' said Mum. 'He didn't know what to make of it all. He obviously doesn't like any kind of violence.'

'Well, neither do I, really,' said Mike, thinking of Bazzer and Gay.

As they said good-night, Nik shook hands with everyone and thanked them for a most interesting and unusual day.

'I enjoyed both battles,' he said.

'Both?'

'Yes, the big one and the little one between Mr Castle

and the large lady.'

Mr Castle held his hands clasped over his head in a gesture of victory.

'*Je suis le champignon.*' he declared.

'Er, Dad,' murmured Mike, 'I think you mean *le champion. Bonsoir,* anyway.'

Mike leaned back in bed, smiling to himself. He picked up his pencil and wrote:

'Dad's not too bad, really, except at French. The cannon was superb all day. Dave is restoring the other one and has invited me over to help. Nik was really interested. I think he enjoyed it. Mum says Pascal was very worried about the fighting. He doesn't seem to understand about anything that's pretend.' He thought for a moment. 'Imagination,' he continued, 'that's what he can't understand. That must be why he couldn't understand jokes at first. He's getting the idea, though. Mum says he was worried in case I got hurt.' He yawned and his eyes closed. 'Pascal is a good mate,' he began, but the day's strenuous activities overcame him and he slept. Not in a seventeenth-century ditch beside the road from Naseby but on clean sheets under a comfortable duvet.

Pascal was fiddling reluctantly with the chain on his wrist and the Senior who appeared on the screen was wearing a look Pascal had never observed before on any Senior's face.

'Today,' he said, 'what happened? What time zone were you in? What was the purpose? Why was the action unreal? Or was it a real conflict? Who were they? Tell me what happened.'

'Don't ask,' said Pascal.

The Senior looked at him sharply. The boy's eyelids were beginning to flutter in the alien fashion.

'I have been asking these questions myself,' Pascal murmured sleepily. Then he smiled very slightly. 'I say to myself, "What on Earth happened?"'

The Senior stared hard at him.

'Tonight,' he said crisply, 'you should sleep immediately. At once.'

'*Bonsoir*,' said Pascal, still smiling.

Chapter Ten

MIKE SPENT the rest of the holiday occupied with the two big problems in his life: Pascal's secret and Bazzer and Gav. Strangely, Pascal was the lesser problem. He was very skilful at avoiding direct contact with Nik.

'No, no,' he would reprove when Nik burst into French, 'we must speak English. That is why we are here.'

'You're a little slave-driver,' Liz would say affectionately. 'Try again, Nik, I'll help you.' He did not actually need all that much help but they both seemed to enjoy it.

Mum's final whirl of hospitality kept other problems at bay. They went to London, visited historic monuments, became tourists themselves.

'Funny how you never go to these places until you've got guests,' said Dad, looking shattered.

Mike arrived home too late and too tired, often, to even write up his diary.

Then there was just one full day left. Tomorrow, Nik would go to the airport and Pascal would go to the station, and it would all be over. Except for Bazzer and Gav.

Mike got slowly out of bed. He walked into the kitchen to find things were happening. Liz was showing Nik and Pascal how to prepare what she called an old-fashioned English breakfast. Mr and Mrs Castle, loud in the boys' praises, were tucking into bacon and mush-rooms.

'I said it must be something simple,' said Pascal solemnly but Mike thought he winked. Pascal was getting the idea about jokes.

'Have you seen this in the paper?' asked Dad. 'That new theme park is open at last. It says "Encyclo-WhoopeeWorld, Where Education is Fun for all the Family".'

'Really?' said Liz. 'I can imagine.'

'It might be better than its name,' said Mum, 'and it would be somewhere to go for your last outing. Why don't you make a day of it and take a packed lunch?'

'I'll do it,' said Mike and Liz, rising simultaneously and getting jammed between the table and the refrigerator in their haste to forestall Mum.

'Great,' said Mum. 'You're a pair of treasures.'

A hint of suspicion stirred in Mike's brain. They had never helped much with the cooking before Mum started her adventurous experiments. Now, they were all volunteering . . .

'A place like that is bound to have a good café, anyway, *mes amis*,' said Dad. 'You could *mangez* a *gateau* or *deux*?'

'Bravo!' said Nik. '*Vous parlez français.*'

'There you are!' said Dad, triumphantly. 'Told you so.'

The theme park was very new indeed. It had been built on the site of an abandoned gravel pit and news of its progress had filled the local papers. The owners had given the impression that it was a mellow blend of fun-fair and reference library. Mike could picture the 'Your Body: the Greatest Adventure' Pavilion. Yes, there had to be people in character costumes everywhere, but they would be Genes or Right Ventricles. He imagined boat trips down the alimentary canal with health education voice-overs. He was rather looking forward to it.

He was not so wrong, either. They made their first stop the Science Pavilion. 'The Wonderful Treasures of the Universe – They Belong to Us All' it said.

'Huh!' snorted Liz. 'Didn't stop them charging us to come in.'

They were looking at the displays and working models when they were accosted by Minnie Molecule herself, a rotund object who urged them into the Science Theatre to see a living demonstration of the action of molecules.

Mike stared in disbelief. Up on the stage were the Molecules, 'cute kids' in costume demonstrating molecular theory through song and dance. Liz was staring, too.

'I know some of them,' she said. 'They're from the Peggy LaRoche School of Dancing. You know, over the chip shop.'

'Let's get out,' said Mike. As he spoke, one little Molecule tripped over her feet and set off a chain reaction, 'Before there's an explosion,' he added. 'This lot could destroy the world.'

As they crept out and into the main hall again, Mike heard a dry, choking noise from Pascal. He realized that Pascal was actually laughing.

'What's up?' he asked, half anxious. Then he understood. 'You're transmitting, aren't you!'

Pascal nodded. 'All of it. It will be very educational for the Seniors. I think this will be my best day.'

So they went to the Space Hall. Pascal would study each display with close attention and then lean on Mike, shaking. Liz was intrigued.

'Pascal's got the giggles,' she said, laughing herself.

They went aboard a space-capsule simulator and were taken on a journey round the planets. This seemed to sober Pascal up a bit. He looked quite green when they came out.

The House of History relied on actors to convey the right atmosphere. 'See the Most Dramatic Moments of History Re-enacted.' Mike wondered about the other moments and expressed doubts about the educational soundness of the project. Short scenes succeeded each other. Queen Elizabeth I waved graciously and Nik, experienced in these matters after Naseby, waved back. Mary Queen of Scots appeared in a ginger wig. As the axe fell on her neck, the lights were extinguished. When they came up again, the body was separated from its distinctly waxy head by several metres.

'Ah, I see,' said Nik. 'I understand this so important moment of British history. If the lights had not failed, she would still be alive today.'

Pascal started laughing again.

The Natural History enclosure was infested by people in gorilla suits. Mike offered one a banana but it told him to push off. They had their packed lunch in a jungle clearing, taking care to put their litter in the special bins, which said 'EncycloWhoopeeWorld invites you to protect the Earth by using this bin'. Pascal made himself dizzy by going round and round the bin, reading the message.

It cost extra to go down the Amazon in a boat but Nik

offered to pay. Liz was especially delighted to meet some friends from school on board and lost no time in introducing Nik to them all. Mike and Pascal hung over the sides, listening to the commentary. Real parrots flew overhead in one section and the boat brushed against the greenery. 'Few men,' said the voice, 'set foot in this green wilderness, remote even from the jungle inhabitants.' A parrot landed on a branch in front of the boys. 'Poor Cyril,' it said. 'Have a cup of tea.' The journey ended in a short stretch of tunnel, as it had begun.

Mike and Pascal went to sit on the log seats while Liz detached herself from her friends. She and Nik came over at last and flopped down on the grass. Nik pulled his programme out of his pocket.

'Next?' he said. 'We have not seen Little Disneyworld, or the MultiTheme Eatery. What is that? Or Wild West City. There is a Show-down and Shoot-out at 4 p.m.'

'Not that,' said Mike quickly. 'Reminds me too much of Bazzer and Gav.'

'Are you still worried?' Liz was angry. 'I could kill that Bazzer.'

'There is a problem?' asked Nik. 'Tell me.'

Mike was silent but Liz told Nik everything.

'He's just hounding Mike and Pascal, the bully. And as for Gav, he should be here in a gorilla suit.'

'You think they will attack you?' Nik asked the question seriously.

'I don't really know.' Mike shrugged. 'They seem to be looking for me. Well, it's Bazzer, really. Gav just does what Bazzer tells him. I don't know what to do.'

'You must go to him,' said Pascal.

No one spoke.

'You mean I should look for him?' asked Mike at last.
'Yes,' said Pascal. 'You must take the initiative. Go and
ask him what he intends to do. As he does not like
French people,' Pascal gave a little smile, 'I will go too.'

'So will I!' roared Nik.

'No,' said Pascal, 'just Mike and Bazzer. I do not
count, really.'

'But you can't take those two yobs on, Mike,' objected Liz.

'Well, then,' said Nik. 'I will find this Gav and talk to
him a little.' He sprang to his feet and executed a few
graceful but powerful movements.

'You seem to have had some training,' said Mike
morosely. 'I haven't.' He looked at Pascal.

'Together? You and I?' suggested Pascal, gently.

'OK,' said Mike. 'I don't know if I'll get out of it in
one piece but I can't go on hiding.'

'OK,' repeated Nik. He seemed enthusiastic. 'We set it
up – that is the right words, is it not? – for tonight!'

Chapter Eleven

EVERYONE KNEW where to find Gav in the evenings. He went to the take-away on a regular basis. Bazzer gave him the money and was thus saved the fatigue of queuing for his supper. Gav would carry the parcel quickly down to the recreation ground where Bazzer was waiting, ready to grumble if it was cold. Tonight, however, Gav did not get as far as joining the queue. Liz and Nik approached him as he turned the corner.

'Gav!' said Liz. 'We've been waiting for you.'

'What?' said Gav, suspiciously.

'You remember me, don't you? Mike Castle's sister. I want to introduce you to Nik here.'

Gav stepped back, glancing round. Nik projected his most charming smile.

'I want to apologize, old boy. For not being your idea of a Frenchman, for not looking like a frog.'

Gav snarled and pushed Nik aside. The next moment, Gav was facing the other way and Nik was propelling him round the corner. The queue heard the apologetic tones fading into the distance.

'No, really, it's all my fault. We really should try harder to look all alike. My father is tall, you see. Looks frightfully English . . .'

Bazzer's supper would be late.

Mike and Pascal made a less impressive couple. They

also knew where to go. Normally, Mike would never have gone anywhere near the rec at night. It was not well lit and the metal gate clanging behind them sounded like a prison door. They stood still and listened. Dogs barking, distant traffic and the slow squeaking of a swing.

'About time, too.' It was Bazzer's voice.

They walked to the swings.

'It's me,' said Mike.

'Castle? And the frog! Well, well.' He stood up slowly and Mike realized that he was surprised. 'What do you want?'

'I thought you wanted me. I thought we'd better get it over and done with.'

'Sorry you were so cheeky, eh?'

'No. I was right,' he said bravely. (I'm also mad, he thought.) 'You just go around spoiling things for other people. I wasn't hurting you. You just picked on us.'

Bazzer raised his hand and hit Mike hard across the face. Mike felt as if all his teeth had moved one place to the right. His skin burned and his eyes watered, but he did not move.

'You see?' Pascal was almost whispering, but his words were clear. 'You can only break. Mike can build. He has built a friendship with me. You can do nothing to Mike, nothing that really matters.'

Mike held his breath. He was afraid of what Bazzer might do to Pascal. Then a voice called across from the gate.

'Bazzer, here we are. Here we all are, at last.'

Liz and Nik were trotting across the grass, arm in arm with Gav. Apart from the look on Gav's face, they might have been three old friends having a good night out together.

'We've brought him. Naughty old Gav!' said Liz.

'Let go of her hand,' snapped Bazzer.

'I'm not,' protested Gav. 'I haven't. I mean, she's got *me*.'

'Oh dear,' said Liz, looking at Mike's face. 'Have you been hitting my little brother? Would you like to hit me? Go on.' She put her face very close to Bazzer's. 'It's quite safe. I won't hit back.' She sounded dangerous.

'Or hit me,' said Nik, cheerfully, 'because I'm French. But I do hit back.'

Bazzer was angry but he also seemed confused. He preferred to choose his own scenarios.

'Let's go,' he snarled at Gav. 'You look ridiculous.' Nik released Gav who shuffled after Bazzer and they heard the gate clang behind them.

'He's the real victim, pathetic old Gav,' said Liz. 'More than you'll ever be,' she added, gently touching Mike's aching face.

'They left the field of battle,' announced Nik, 'so we are the winners, no?' He crossed his hands and shook Mike's and Pascal's at the same time.

'All for one and one for all,' shouted Liz. 'You recognize that, don't you?'

'Yes, of course,' said Nik, 'it comes from an American film. Now for the famous English chips.'

'Last day of this strange exchange,' wrote Mike, the following night. 'It's all over. Dad and Liz took Nik to the airport. He said he had really enjoyed himself. He wants us all to go over for the next holidays. He said Dad shouldn't waste his talent for French.

'Pascal and I went over to Grandad's for the last meal because he said he had something for Pascal. It was the photo of Pascal holding the rabbit, with me and Liz grinning in the background. I nearly gave the game away. 'Will you be able to take it back?' I asked. 'Of course he will,' said Grandad, 'it weighs nothing.' Pascal said, 'I will take it and keep it for ever.' I think he will.

'Mum didn't insist on coming to the station. We were all a bit sad, so there it was, just Pascal and me. We said goodbye outside the station as Pascal said I wouldn't see him go. I gave him a book as a present. It seems terribly final. Think I'll go and see Grandad tomorrow.

'Pascal gave me a present as well. It was the bronze link from his chain. He daren't give me the whole chain and he doesn't know how powerful the bronze link is on its own. He says he likes our word 'link' which can mean two things. If he finds out how to contact me, I think he will.

'It's funny, but I'm not afraid of Bazzer and Gav any-more. Anyway, if there's any more trouble, I'll just men-tion Liz's name. Gav looked really embarrassed.

'I'm just going to record what we had for tea tonight in case there's an enquiry. We had Kidney Alaska. I think this has something to do with not helping in the house and I'm going to tackle Mum. I shall say, 'Look here, Mum, how will you feel when the coroner opens me up and finds all this stuff? Why are you doing it?' It's time to call her bluff.'

Mike put his pencil down and sighed. Then his mouth twitched and he picked it up again.

'PS. Mum did some hoovering for Grandad when we were over there. I think she was feeling a bit upset, too, because she fixed the hose to the wrong end. Dust blew everywhere. It was hurricane conditions. I don't know why, but Pascal laughed like a drain. Really laughed. I'll miss him.'

'Welcome back, Young One,' said the Senior. 'You are to go to the transmission screen at once.'

Pascal walked down the corridor and into the communication cabin. He sat down in front of the screen which was already alive. The Head of Mission himself was waiting to interview him.

'You are well? No ill effects?'

'I am well.'

'You will report to the medical staff as soon as this interview is over. You must be thoroughly checked.'

'I understand.'

'You know we have abandoned the mission?'

'Yes, I know. I have failed.'

'Failed? Why do you say that? Nonsense. You have sent valuable data. We were right, you see, in a way. Only one as young as yourself could get near to the human mind, and you showed us that our analysis was incomplete. There is much to learn about humans. You have taught us that.'

'I changed.'

'Yes, a little. I must admit we did not realize that they would be as powerful as that. And the rituals, – so surprising. The earth, air, fire and water ritual was completed, I believe, as we predicted?'

Pascal paused.

'Yes, Sir. The air element was performed today. It is called "hoovering".'

'Hoovering? But I know this "hoovering". It is a cleaning process.'

'Not if the tube is put on the wrong end. It then blows instead of sucks.'

'I see.' The Senior looked doubtful but dismissed the problem for the moment. 'Anything else of immediate importance? You will be properly debriefed later.'

'My friends gave me two gifts. I should like to keep them.'

'I see. Well, this mission has been an important part of your life. I understand that. What are the gifts?'

'A photograph.'

'Hold it up to the screen. Yes, fascinating indeed. A copy for archives, please. And the other?'

'A book, Sir.'

'Splendid. We must have a copy of that, too. Books always reveal culture. What is it called?'

'*The Mega Ho-Ho Joke Book*, Sir,' Pascal said blissfully.

Barn Owl Books

THE PUBLISHING HOUSE DEVOTED ENTIRELY TO
THE REPRINTING OF CHILDREN'S BOOKS

RECENT TITLES

Arabel's Raven — Joan Aiken

Mortimer the raven is determined to sleep in the bread bin. Mrs Jones says no

Mortimer's Bread Bin — Joan Aiken

Mortimer the raven finds the Joneses and causes chaos in Rumbury Town

The Spiral Stair — Joan Aiken

Giraffe thieves are about! Arabel and her raven have to act fast

The Secret Summer of Daniel Lyons — Roy Apps

Tom pretends to be Daniel Lyons, so that he can spend a summer working on a film

Your Guess is as Good as Mine — Bernard Ashley

Nicky gets into a stranger's car by mistake

The Gathering — Isobelle Carmody

Four young people and a ghost battle with a strange evil force

Voyage — Adèle Geras

Story of four young Russians sailing to the U.S. in 1904

Private — Keep Out! — Gwen Grant

Diary of the youngest of six in the 1940s

Leila's Magical Monster Party — Ann Jungman
Leila invites all the baddies to her party and they come!

The Silver Crown — Robert O'Brien
A rare birthday present leads to an extraordinary quest

Playing Beatie Bow — Ruth Park
Exciting Australian time travel story in which Abigail learns about love

The Mustang Machine — Chris Powling
A magic bike sorts out the bullies

The Phantom Carwash — Chris Powling
When Lenny asks for a carwash for Christmas, he doesn't expect to get one, never mind a magic one.

The Intergalactic Kitchen — Frank Rodgers
The Bird family plus their kitchen go into outer space

You're Thinking about Doughnuts — Michael Rosen
Frank is left alone in a scary museum at night

Jimmy Jelly — Jacqueline Wilson
A T.V. personality is confronted by his greatest fan

The Devil's Arithmetic — Jane Yolen
Hannah from New York time travels to Auschwitz in 1942 and acquires wisdom